Keith David Pratt lives with his wife, in a small village in Essex. He has two grown up daughters and three grand children.

He started his career operating and programming mainframe computers, this developed into a role where he needed to analyse the business problems that needed new systems. He realised that his skills were focused primarily in IT, so with the help of The Open University Business School he attained a Master of Business Administration degree (MBA).

Keith relaxes sailing, and has an RYA yacht master certificate.

My wife and family
Steve Hardy
Nick Webb

Keith David Pratt

OTHER MAN'S GRASS

AUSTIN MACAULEY PUBLISHERS™

LONDON • CAMBRIDGE • NEW YORK • SHARJAH

A CIP catalogue record for this title is available from the British Library.

ISBN 9781398457416 (Paperback)
ISBN 9781398457423 (ePub e-book)

www.austinmacauley.com

First Published 2022
Austin Macauley Publishers Ltd®
1 Canada Square
Canary Wharf
London
E14 5AA

To Austin Macauley Publishers Ltd.

Chapter 1

Rita was in a deep sleep when the alarm sounded. Her sleep had been interrupted earlier when Paul's alarm had sounded, she still felt tired. She lazily reached out and pressed the snooze button to give herself ten more minutes to rouse from her sleepy state. She realised when the alarm sounded again that this was not a good move; it seemed only seconds since the alarm had first sounded. She decided to sit up, with her legs over the side of the bed, to turn the alarm off this time.

Still sitting on the bed, her brain slowly started to take control, her demeanour enlightened, realising that it was Friday.

Today she felt strong, in control and needed. She knew that there had been too many years, since her unexpected pregnancy and marriage to Paul, that she had not had these positive feelings. She realised that she was as much to blame as Paul for the way their marriage had become monotonous.

She remembered when she first met Paul how infatuated she was by his presence and how she dressed and applied her makeup to impress him. At the beginning of their relationship, she felt that being with Paul was more special than any other boyfriend she had previously been dating. As a teenager she did not realise, until she met Paul, that she was subconsciously judging her dates as potential partners. When she had been in a conversation with her friends about their recent dates, she realised that she was completely different from them. She soon realised that all her friends needed were light-hearted fun from the boys they went on a date with and all she needed was a secure loving partner. Now as an older woman she realised that this related to her own upbringing by her parents.

She stood up from the bed and moved over to the full-length mirror door of the wardrobe and studied herself in her silk nightdress, which she felt good wearing, as she slowly slid her hand down her thigh, she liked how it felt as well. She was thinking that now in her forties she was still quite attractive. Her face had very few wrinkles. Her eyes were still fresh and bright. Her hairstyle made her face look younger. Her analytical focus moved down to her legs, at the same time, holding her silk nightdress with both hands on her thighs, she lifted it to reveal more of her naked legs of which she still felt were attractive. She realised that her attention to diet and exercise at the local gym continued to pay her back.

Her thoughts flashed back to her husband, married now for over twenty years, she could not remember the last time he had complimented her on the way she looks, all she could remember was his sarcastic comments about the food she prepared and the inconvenience, to him, of the time that she spent at the gym and the cost of her beauty treatments. It was these underlying tones of how much she cost to keep that had made her decide, when Lottie their daughter, had left school and started university that she would go back to work.

She knew that working in the city had restored her independence; she enjoyed the luxuries that Paul's income provided but her independence was now paramount after the time spent loving and raising their daughter, plus she had grown her job to include higher responsibility.

She slid her nightdress up and over her head and then stared at her naked body congratulating herself on how flat her tummy was at her age after carrying a baby. She studied her breasts knowing that they were not as pert as they were before feeding Lottie but to her, they still looked passable.

After looking out of the bedroom window she decided that it was going to be another warm June day. So, she opened the wardrobe and took out her favourite thin cotton dress. Then she opened her underwear draw and took out the bra and panties that she knew looked good, made her feel good and would make him feel good, and went with her cotton dress.

Chapter 2

Lottie sat in the living room in the armchair shaping her nails with an emery board thinking how happy she felt about the sacrifices her mother and father had made to raise her and to guide her in the right direction. She also reflected on their reaction when she and Kevin had told them of their pregnancy, supportive as they had ever been, but later more inquisitive about the plan they had both shared to start a family. Lottie and Kevin felt that eventually they had convinced them that all was going to plan and that getting pregnant this time was just the start.

She could hardly believe that this was real. Only last Friday she was in her office, in the publishing company where she worked, making sure her assistant had all the information she needed for the books that were being published in the next six months. Lottie and Kevin's baby was due in six weeks' time.

The local radio station was playing "The way we were" by Gladys Knight. Lottie looked at her perfectly shaped nails thinking that this may be very relevant for Kevin and me when our baby arrives. Her mind wandered to thoughts of the nursery room in their two-bed roomed apartment in Inner London when the news report started on the radio.

"There has been a stabbing of a teenage boy in Gresham Road last night, stay tuned for more details." Lottie drew in a large gasp of breath; Gresham Road was five minutes' walk away from their apartment. The report continued saying that two teenagers were being held in custody and were being questioned about the incident.

Thoughts about how the teenage victim's parents must be feeling flooded her mind mixed with thoughts about how she would feel as she gently wrapped her hands around her unborn child.

She closed her eyes. Unexpectedly she dossed, her legs on the outstretched leg rest, with the armchair slightly reclined, a lovely present from Kevin. When Kevin had been at the "Fathers to be" meeting the midwife told them that they must allow their partners to rest regularly before the birth of their child. Kevin, as usual, went a stage further, hence the chair.

Lottie awoke suddenly when she heard the apartment entrance door banging closed. As she opened her eyes the living room door opened and Kevin walked in, more purposefully than normal, apologising profusely when he realised that he had disturbed Lottie in her comfy armchair.

The thought crashed through his mind that if the midwife had been here to witness this stupid act, he would have lost serious "Father to be" team points.

"I am really sorry darling," Kevin said in a low soft voice, "I am home early and didn't think ahead enough to realise it would be your rest time sorry darling."

"Don't keep saying sorry Kevin, I am more concerned about why you are home early," Lottie replied enquiringly. There was a brief silence as a broad smile filled Kevin's face.

"I have been promoted and they let me off early to tell my lovely pregnant lady in person," Kevin replied.

"Oh, that's brilliant darling, at last they have realised how hard you work," was Lottie's instant reply.

"Well yes, but it could also have something to do with the fact that I am quite good at what I do as well," Kevin added sheepishly.

"Does this mean a salary increase?" Lottie said in a voice they both knew was mimicking her Publisher boss.

"Yes," was Kevin's simple answer, followed by a long pause, making an excited Lottie slide into her sarcastic communication mode as she said, "So you are not going to tell me how much then? OK, as you know I cannot live with a partner who does not share honesty, so your baby and I will be......."

"25% of my current salary," Kevin interrupted.

"Oh, a cut not a raise," Lottie continued sarcastically.

Then cuddling Kevin, she said, "25% more, they must think you are good at what you do." After kissing him she said "And so do I, but not only at work. So, I am going to cook us a celebratory dinner."

As Lottie was preparing the food her mind was racing. Today was a day of bad news and good news, are they linked she wondered. While Lottie was in the kitchen Kevin sat scribbling numbers into his notebook, smiling as he did so.

"Perfectly cooked as usual," Kevin said in a formal way as he placed his knife and fork on his empty plate. "Now we must do some extra work together,"

"Oh, so cooking isn't considered work then," Lottie retorted jokingly, "What work?" she added.

"Identifying somewhere, not more than twenty miles away close to a railway station, where we can bring up our family," Kevin said smiling.

"What? Move home?" said Lottie.

"Why don't you want to move home?" Kevin said seriously.

"Yes, I do, Inner London has been fine for us as a business couple but as a family, and after the news this morning."

"What news?" asked Kevin.

Lottie explained and when she had finished Kevin said he would go and get the map so that they could identify suitable places that fitted their criteria and that they would go and visit at the weekend.

Kevin then placed his hands tenderly on Lottie's stomach saying, "We have agreed we need to bring you up in a safe stable environment."

Hearing her son-in-law may have had an influence on Rita's future if she had heard him.

Chapter 3

David stood behind her, his arm loosely around her waist. With his other hand he gently uncovered her tender perfumed neck. He softly kissed her, moving slowly towards her shoulder, she quietly sighed in response. He moved her fair hair to continue kissing her other shoulder, she sighed again. He did not rush, and moved to the top of her back, that was exposed by her delicate summer dress. Kissing her neck, he slowly undid the zip at the back of her dress, he then slid both hands under the shoulder straps and gently caressing her shoulders the dress fell seductively to the floor. She smoothly turned, looked into his strong eyes, and kissed his lips, gently at first, and then with one of her slim manicured hands on either side of David's face, both kissed the other more strongly. Their tongues shared sensual penetration and discovery. David could feel her slowly undoing his shirt buttons, he dropped his arms and his shirt fell coquettishly to the floor beside her summer dress. As her hands undid his trousers, he kissed her neck and moved the straps of her bra over her shoulders.

Although both of their hearts were racing with excitement neither wanted to increase the speed of this intense act of love.

Their naked bodies embraced provocatively. David kissed her mouth then her neck and slowly releasing his embrace he kissed her erect nipples. He continued, her cleavage, her soft stomach, he explored her belly button with his tongue, then kneeling he moved to her pubic mound and below. She reacted by gently placing her hands on his head and opening her legs.

As David stood, he slid his hands up the outside of her legs, lifting her as he reached the swelling of her soft bottom. He pulled her towards him as he penetrated her.

"I am so pleased for two reasons," she said as they were both getting dressed.

"The first is that I am so pleased that everyone in your office goes home at two o'clock on a Friday, plus you use an office with no windows and a solid oak door."

"That I remembered to lock, this time, before we got carried away," David added with a broad smile.

David reached out and held both of her hands, kissing her fingers lightly, "Rita I find your presence so stimulating you make me feel and act like a teenager, but as we are both over forty years of age, we must try to control our lust for each other until we are alone together in a less public place," David said as he cuddled her and smelt her intoxicating perfume.

"Yes, we need to be together more," she said studying her caressed fingers, adding "I'm ready for that move now David."

But Rita did not know what this commitment would entail.

Chapter 4

Jeff replaced the telephone handset and slumped into the armchair with his clenched fist hard against his forehead.

"Oh shit," he said aloud thinking that his daughter Rita had done exactly what her mother had done to him. He could not contemplate that Rita had left Paul.

The only way Jeff could console himself was that Rita needed to let her father know on the same day that she had walked out of the marriage. He had been so stunned during the conversation that he now realised that he had not asked Rita whether she had told Lottie her own daughter. Jeff thought what a great piece of news for a pregnant granddaughter.

"Oh shit!" he exclaimed again when he remembered that Rita had called when he was getting ready for work. The thought of driving an articulated lorry at night after news like this did not fill him with enthusiasm. I am sixty-three next year and need peace for my pending retirement, not family upheaval.

On the way to the depot, he came to his own conclusions, both his wife Joan and his daughter Rita had become pregnant as teenagers and that he and Paul had supported the unexpected family, forcing him to think that if they had not made the mistake and fallen pregnant that they would not have accepted marriage from himself or Paul.

He climbed into the driving seat at the depot, put the key into the ignition but before starting the engine he decided that he needed to clear his mind regarding Rita's announcement and concentrate on driving a forty-foot articulated lorry, a death machine if not driven correctly. He could not clear his mind completely but felt more comfortable to start the lorry and his night trucking duties.

As Jeff left the depot, he decided that tonight he was going to stick to his normal routine, so he headed for the late-night transport café. As he approached, he could see from the parked Lorries that the normal crew were there, he decided quickly that he was not going to share his news.

Jeff made his usual purchase at the counter, large mug of tea and a cheese roll and went to sit at the usual table with George, Dave, and Jock. George and Dave were not visible behind the Evening Standard newspapers they were reading so only Jock acknowledged Jeff's arrival.

From behind his paper George suddenly spoke, "I reckon I could do better meself a goalmouth the size of the Blackwall tunnel and what does he do, trips over his own bloody feet and fall flat on his face." Dave from behind the other paper replied, "Yeh paid a bloody fortune and can't stay on their own two feet either on the pitch or in their private lives, I'd like to see them doing our bloody job."

Dave folds his paper, nods at Jeff, and asks George, "Who did you play on Saturday?"

"The Labour," George replied as he folded his paper also nodding at Jeff.

Jeff suddenly thought these guys are younger than my daughter I should be retired already.

Jock suddenly joined in the conversation, "What? The party?"

"No dickhead, the exchange, the blokes on the dole," was the stern reply from George.

"They beat us. They were as good as last year cos the team hadn't bloody changed. I am sure they all don't want jobs cos they all want to stay in the winning team."

Jeff sat listening to the football conversation but found it hard to stop thinking about the impact Rita's move was going to have on the family.

Chapter 5

Paul sat at the traffic lights in his Mercedes on his way home from work, the windows were open both sides at the front as it had been a hot June day and was still warm. Passing by on the pavement was a woman on her own, probably in her late fifties, talking to herself rather loudly. Paul started to feel a little sorry for her when he realised that she was talking into a small microphone attached to a wire that disappeared under her hair, blast he thought a mobile phone.

"You are supposed to be a senior person working in Information Technology," he said to himself.

"Why shouldn't an older person use the latest technology?"

A crazy end to a crazy week he thought.

Suddenly he felt his blood energy and life being sucked out of him again; he couldn't think how many times this had happened to him since Sunday.

On Sunday whilst he was sitting in the study going through the project implementation plan for the following week Rita came in and stood at the side of his desk. There was a period of silence; Paul thought this is strange she has never been interested in my work before. Paul looked up at her, she put her hand on his shoulder and said, "Paul I am sorry, but I don't love you anymore and today, now, I am leaving you."

Paul's disbelief of the statement made him say, "OK darling what have I done wrong this time, spending too much time on this important, lucrative project."

Rita replied calmly and monotonically, "I don't want to talk about it now, I have written you a note it is in the lounge please read it when I've gone."

Rita turned, left the study, opened the front door, closed it quietly, got into her car and drove away slowly. Paul thought this is an unusual mode of winding me up she has never used this one before, thinking it was probably discussed last night when she was having one of her many girls' nights out, he had suffered Rita's friends schemes before. He spent a short while longer ensuring that he had covered all the detail in the project plan for next week's crucial implementation after all it was the customer who gave him the best paying projects. He finished and went down to the kitchen to make himself a cup of coffee wondering where Rita had gone and how long she would be. With his mug of coffee, he went into the Lounge. On the shelf over the fireplace was a white envelope with Paul in Rita's handwriting on the front. He put his mug on a coaster on the small coffee table, one of Rita's requirements, strategically placed coasters he thought, picked up the envelope and opened it. There were three sheets of A4 handwritten paper inside, he sat and started to read.

Chapter 6

Kevin helped Lottie clear the dining table and load the dish washer, which they had started to use again when they read that it used less energy than washing dishes by hand, they were both very interested in recycling and saving global energy.

When the table was clear Kevin unfolded his large map and went to the cupboard and found his compasses. He checked the scale of the map and set his largest compass to equal twenty miles on the scale. Being in the I.T. profession for so long had made Kevin accurate at everything he did. Lottie loved him for this quality but every now and again it frustrated her, and she described him as being small minded and slow. Hence her comment when she approached him at the table after he had drawn a pencil circle on the map around inner London where they lived.

"It doesn't need to be exactly twenty miles, there may be a perfect village twenty-one miles from where we live now."

"OK darling, but don't knock it, my attention to detail was why I was promoted today." They both laughed and Lottie gave Kevin a tender kiss.

After studying the map, with the pencil circle, for a while they both agreed that doing it this way helped them identify the distance of the mainline stations as well as the distance of schools, hospitals, and the main towns. They had both felt, before they started, that they would be able to identify a few places that met their criteria. But, after studying the map for some time they were both attracted to just one village, Amberton.

There was a mainline station at Redford, which was just a couple of miles away, and Redford had a hospital and schools and looked like a reasonable sized town. They discussed it together and it seemed that they were both being drawn to Amberton for no reason they could fully understand.

Lottie started smiling and chuckling to herself. "Why are you so happy darling is it something that I have done or said," Kevin enquired.

"No nothing like that Kevin, it's just that we seem to have been guided to choose Amberton," Lottie replied, still smiling looking up with her hand pointing to the ceiling.

"Yes, my darling," Kevin said sarcastically, "maybe the ceiling can guide us on getting a mortgage as we don't know how expensive houses in Amberton are going to be."

"All right Kevin, I know you don't believe in the way that I feel that my life is being guided," Lottie said softly.

"I do thank your guide for telling you to say Yes when I called you for our first date," Kevin replied jokingly. They both laughed as they cuddled, looking at the map on their dining room table.

The phone rang and Lottie answered it. All Kevin could hear was Lottie's reply mainly consisting of "Oh, if that is what you feel is best." Lottie replaced the receiver slowly; Kevin knew that something was wrong and had to interrupt Lottie's quiet reflection.

"Was that bad news darling?"

"Yes, upsetting news, my mother and father have separated."

Kevin continued to cuddle Lottie as she slowly digested this unsettling news.

At six o'clock the following morning Lottie was awake. Kevin could sense she was awake and asked if he could do anything to help believing that it might be regarding last night's phone call from her mother. "Yes darling, you could carry our child for the next few weeks as your stomach skin is probably a little thicker than mine as our first born to be is currently running the London Marathon or swimming the English Channel today."

"Oh," Kevin said relieved that the recent news had been replaced, "So our little one is kicking hard today?"

"Just a bit darling," Lottie replied sarcastically clenching her teeth. "Our child is excited that today is the day our family is going to look at a new village and a new house to live in," Kevin said, not knowing what to do to help.

"Well, we had better get up and go to Amberton, or as first-time parents is this giving in to our child's demands too early and too easily," Lottie replied with a broad smile across her face.

"You have been reading too many of those parenting books you used to publish," Kevin said as he got up from bed, heading for the chest of drawers.

They both got ready and went to their car. Kevin had folded the map smaller so that Lottie could tell him what roads to take when they got closer to Amberton as Kevin knew the main road to get within a few miles of Redford.

As Lottie could also drive, she gave Kevin directions well in advance. They soon approached Amberton along one of the four narrow roads leading to the centre indicated by a dot on their map.

The dot was a large village green with a large pond surrounded by a narrow road to which the four approach roads joined. "Well done darling," Kevin praised Lottie, "I could never have found this without a good map reader."

"My father has lost his map reader now." Kevin was now fully aware that the news had not drifted to the back of Lotties mind.

Kevin drove slowly around the village green noticing the village pub, "The Fox and Goose. Maybe we can have lunch there," he suggested to Lottie.

"As long as they serve lunch and not just beer," Lottie replied smiling.

After a couple of circuits of the village green they had discovered the village shop/post office, a quaint primary school and a very old looking Church. They both agreed that they were beginning to fall in love with Amberton.

They had also looked for 'For Sale' signs but had seen none. "Maybe this is such a lovely village that nobody ever moves out," was Lottie's thought that she shared with Kevin. "Let's go to Redford and find an estate agent," was Kevin's logical reply.

Kevin parked in the Redford High Streetcar Park and they walked to the first estate agent that they could find. They gave the manager a brief explanation of why they were in his office including their purchase budget and the fact that they both liked Amberton.

The manager went to a large filing cabinet and returned with details of two properties. Kevin and Lottie looked at each other with surprise because of the lack of signs in Amberton.

The manager handed Lottie one of the property details and Kevin the other. Turning to Lottie he said, "This property is in Amberton, and it only came on the market a couple of days ago and we are the prime agents, in fact you are the first people to be given these details, and it is within your budget." Turning to Kevin he said, "this one is on the outskirts of Redford is very convenient for the mainline station but is five thousand over your budget."

Kevin and Lottie studied the details swapping a couple of times. They both agreed that they would like to view both properties today if possible. The manager said, "The one in Amberton is vacant possession and I have the key so no problem; I must telephone the vendors of the Redford property to see if viewing today is convenient."

Chapter 7

Now regularly, the thought of his wife, Rita, and his friend, David, making love together swamped his thoughts with chilling hurt disbelief and overpowering anger. Where had they done it? Another chill went through his body. His brain raced with thoughts, knitted together, they pointed to the bed in his room at home. Anger again. How could she, they, have done it? Betrayal and despair possessed him. I am not a violent man, he thought, but I would like to see that bastard dead.

Rita took her gym entrance card and gave it to the gym receptionist, whom she did not recognize, making her realise that it had been a few months since she had been to her local gym. Since she had been living in David's house, she had found another branch of her gym just around the corner from where she works in London. David left for work early every morning and usually met Rita at her office to accompany her home. So, Rita was up earlier, having time to always get a seat on the train and call in at her new gym before starting work – quite an advantage.

Walking to the ladies changing room she did recognize something, the musty, pungent smell of male sweat as she passed the male changing room as a man who had just come from the main gym walked in. She realised that the London branch, and her early morning start, had another advantage, that the obnoxious smell did not have time to build up to be so pungent as it was late evening after returning home from work.

She cursed herself for letting herself fall back into her old routine and coming to the gym in the evening after her days work, she also cursed herself because it reminded her of her previous life with Paul and not being cared for as she now feels with David. It had not been an easy day at work either. Her job had continued to grow, in responsibility, even more since she and Paul had separated. She felt her brain had had more exercise than her body so when David had said that the darts team had a match to play at a local pub, she decided that instead of sitting in a crowded pub trying to add up the scores, she would work out at her old gym instead to try to balance her bodies imbalance, plus she felt that alcohol would probably not have the right affect. Plus, the thought that Paul may turn up and make an embarrassing scene with both her and David.

Having finished her workout, she smiled to herself as she decided to finish her visit to her old gym with a visit to the steam sauna room completing the routine she had when she was a regular member. She entered the small door and the dense steam and heat enveloped her immediately. She quickly thought that this was one of the luxuries that she had missed by using the London branch but remembered that she had convinced herself that having a hot sauna before starting work in the morning would not be a good idea. As the only person using the steam room Rita closed her eyes letting the hot atmosphere absorb her. She opened them quickly when the door opened.

"Hello Rita, it has been ages since you have been here, it's great to see you again."

"Oh, hello Sue, no I now go to the London branch before starting work, I have found that the change of gym suits me better." Sue made herself comfortable.

"Yes, from what I hear you have had a few changes lately?"

"Yes, changes for the better I am glad to report, so how is Ian." "Playing darts tonight,"

"Oh, so is David,"

"Yes, they both play for the team in the local pub."

Even in the high heat Rita felt a shiver going down her back as she realised that there was so much, she did not know, that others did know, about David's life and current pastimes.

"So, I suppose you had the invitation, as all the women get, to go and take the scores and you declined, as we all do, and preferred to come to the gym,"

"Yes, brain has been over exercised today and body hasn't."

"Well, I am surprised debonair David has not over exercised your shapely body!"

"Does he still shave with a cutthroat razor to keep his face nice and smooth for kissing?"

Rita was stunned by this statement and did not wish to reply and simply looked at the steam vent as a new cloud started being pumped in. Sue closed her eyes leaning her head against the tiled wall and relaxed in the new cloud of steam. Rita could not relax again, her tired brain continued to churn over Sue's statement particularly the debonair description and she had to guess that Ian had told her about his shaving habit. Yes, David always dressed impeccably and always smelt divine, even sitting in the steam room she could imagine smelling his seductive aftershave. But how much did she not know about David? Because of his friendship with Paul, she had never felt she needed to raise the subject of his interests and activities before they became partners. She had never asked him the reasons why he and his wife had separated she realised that she had only questioned Paul at the time of David's break up and had been told that David's wife had 'gone off with another man' she now accepted that this was a man's perception of the situation. She knew it was not possible, but she would like to talk to David's wife to understand the female reasons for their separation. She then felt guilty as she had never shared her reasons for her separation with Paul with any of her female friends, she had 'gone off with another man' was maybe why Sue had commented as she had.

"I must admit I envy you Rita," was the statement that wafted through the steam.

"Yes, David is a very caring partner," Rita quietly replied thinking about her earlier comment.

"I believe that at our age and having brought up a family and living with the same man for over twenty years we all need more excitement, so I envy you for having the drive to make the break." "Oh," Rita was shocked that Sue was being so openly shameless, a quality she had never witnessed before. Without taking any notice of Rita's brief rebuke, "When Ian and I first met our life was thoroughly packed with exciting events, even having sex in the car in a forest car park because we could not wait to get home to do it. Now the excitement has all gone, so I am mega envious that you have

31

gone and found excitement with David. Maybe one day I will have the guts to do it."

"Oh," was Rita's shocked reply.

"Yes, it gets to a stage in a relationship that physical excitement no longer exists, don't get me wrong, I know our partners try hard to have sex exciting for us and themselves but after a while you know all the moves and it loses its excitement, but doing it with someone new and unknown must recreate that excitement."

Rita simply starred at Sue without comment wondering whether it was the steamy room that was making her perspire heavily or what Sue was saying that she had never heard her say before, they had chatted in the past but never about such intimate personal things. She realised that Sue was on a role, so she decided to simply listen.

"Yes, my theory is that in their younger year's males must demonstrate their masculinity based on how many females they can conquer sexually, so their sexual demand is high, but in later years following marriage and having a family it dwindles rapidly in favour of more practical things such as work and hobbies, or for some a renewed attraction for younger females with more shape and less baggage. But I believe that after bringing up a family, females want to make themselves look attractive to the male gender again. It is great news if this attracts your existing partner, but this is not often the case, so when someone new spends more than the usual amount of time looking at you, and they fit your shopping list of male attractive constituents, there is no stopping the sense of arousal that the encounter creates. Well, it does for me, and I guess it did for you seeing as you are now in an exciting new relationship with David who does have many attractive constituents."

Not knowing what to say Rita simply half smiled tilting her head cautiously to the left away from where Sue sat.

"When I first met Ian, I fell head over heels in love with him, you may have felt the same when you first met Paul."

Rita nods, trying in the current circumstances and steamy environment to be careful and non-committal.

"But as time, family and subtle disagreements happen, the head over heels feeling passes," Sue looks at Rita for approval but continues without acknowledgement.

"I think women are so different from men when falling in love, women become so focused on their chosen man that they disregard most other things around them, whereas men do not seem to do the head over heels thing but concentrate more on the logical approach, I guess this is not what happens in all cases, but it did for me. Ian, I felt, was thinking more about making a long-term commitment to me. That is why I believe women, when head over heels in love, are looking for long term commitment, and because they are so focused on that one relationship and future partner and their partner is trying to please his woman that the men are pressured into not being emotionally in love but logically in love."

Rita placing her left hand on her chin could only reply with, "Mmmmm," before Sue continued.

"From what I understand about our marriages, Ian has looked after me, Paul has looked after you, and David looked after his wife, so why did she leave David, and why have you left Paul, and why am I the odd one out."

Rita realising this was becoming a lot heavier conversation decided to change the subject.

"Sue, I did not see you in the gym earlier, did you go to one of the exercise classes, do they still run them in the evenings here?"

"No, I just came here for a steam tonight," Sue replied still using a thoughtful tone. It quickly crossed Rita's tired brain that Sue may well know why David's wife had left him but she decided that following Sue's tyrannical outburst that this was not the time or place to ask and simply said, "Well it has been good to see you again Sue maybe if we get pressured into scoring at the darts match I will see you again," as she stood and made a quicker than normal exit realising that she had not made eye contact with Sue before leaving and being outside the steam room in the noticeably cooler environment.

In the changing room Rita showered, trying not to get her hair wet, as she could wash and condition it at home before David came home, redressed quickly, and left the gym trying not to make contact with Sue or anyone else that she may know.

The conversation with Sue had made her tired brain even more tired and Rita knew that it was because she had started to ask herself questions that she had never thought of asking herself before the steam room encounter. One question that she knew she must ask herself before David's return was how she would describe the conversation with Sue to David, who almost certainly will talk to Ian about them meeting. She decided that a vague comment like "Oh we just chatted about things that have happened since we last met." Oh, Rita thought, that may not be the right way to go about it, as David and I have happened since we last met, and he is bound to be interested in what friends' wives think.

Rita started to smile to herself as she considered saying, "Well actually Sue took up the whole time telling me how much she wants a very hot lustful affair as Ian does not excite her anymore." She stopped smiling as quickly as she had started, thinking David may ask her if that was why she had moved in with him. Another question she knew she had to ask herself later when she could think straight. She realised how little she knew about David's work and contacts, only his office on a Friday afternoon. What did he do to earn an income that supported his above average lifestyle?

Chapter 8

The sun shining through the bedroom window the following morning waked Paul. As he woke, he realised that he must have returned home late from the local pub the previous night, following the phone conversation that he had with Lottie, which had made him feel like a serious drink. He did remember that he was only a little pissed as he decided not to close the curtains in defiance against Rita, as it was her regular routine. They had heated discussions in the past, her side was that she didn't want to be woken by the sun, and his was that they didn't really need curtains, as they were not overlooked by anyone. As his brain started to function, he realised that it wasn't the sunlight that had woken him but the fact that he had tried to cuddle the silky body that was usually beside him. He suddenly went cold, and his heart started racing as he thought that was probably what David was experiencing right now.

Why hadn't Rita told Lottie that she had left her father to go and live with another man, Paul felt even more confused?

Paul decided to put on his shorts and go and sit in his garden. After the alcohol he had consumed last night, he didn't feel like doing much else. He felt strongly about sitting on the decking that he had paid a local company to erect at the back of the house for Rita last summer, just one of the many things that she had said would be good to have that he had provided for her. He also decided that "hair of the dog" would be a good move, so he poured himself a San Miguel, he loved Spanish beer it reminded him of Fuerteventura where he had bought an apartment. Another Rita "would be good to have" statement.

As he sat sipping his beer, he could feel the early morning sun softly bathing his face, he could smell the flowers and bushes waking to the warmth of the sun's rays. He looked over the hedge at the bottom of his garden at the farm field adjoining. The wheat – well he thought it was wheat that James was growing (he should have asked him last night when he was drinking with him at the local) – was moving very gently as the light breeze passed over it. Then a sudden shiver went through him again, he had nobody to share these special moments in his life with anymore. He questioned himself, had he shared these moments or not, her letter implied that he had not.

Paul went and got another beer from the fridge and started to wish that he had never torn up and threw away Rita's note. He was deeply hurt and angry, when reading it, especially when he read that she was going to live with David whose divorce had only been finalized about a year ago.

He sat back on the decking and thought hard about her accusation that he did not show her that he loved her anymore, that they didn't do things together like they had in the early years of their marriage and that he seemed to enjoy his work more than he enjoyed being with her which was the main reason she had given Lottie for their separation. He remembered, that when reading it this is where his anger started to grow. Yes, he thought, I do enjoy the challenges my work provides but the stimulating motivation was not to satisfy my ego but to provide a better than average lifestyle for Rita, Lottie, and himself which the note had not appeared to take into consideration.

Paul continued to think about the note and the overall situation, the beautiful day and the surrounding wildlife palled into insignificance. So, in the last few months, he considered, Rita had not said in her note how long the affair with David had been going on for, David had been giving her the attention that he had not had the time to show her, couldn't she sense that all he wanted to do was get inside her knickers. But Paul continued to analyse it further. David is a city broker so when the market closes the only reason that he would not be home at the same time would be because of a fault with trains, he didn't have an all-hour's workload like me, Paul thought. Although Paul had been friends with David for several years, he had no knowledge of David's unofficial dealings which kept him occupied outside office hours. But from time to time he couldn't make the darts matches.

In the past David had never shared the reasons behind his wife leaving, but Paul did remember that it was for another man. So, Paul felt hurt by his now ex-friend taking his wife and thought, how could he have done this to me when he must have felt the same when someone took his wife. "Oh shit," he said to himself, "perhaps that is where I have been misjudging the situation, do I really feel that wives are possessions?" perhaps this was a lesson David learnt after his wife left him. Paul realised that his thoughts were becoming very mixed up, probably because of his alcohol consumption, but because he didn't have any distraction, his brain and his overwhelming uncontrollable thoughts had taken over and stopped him thinking logically.

He got up, unsteadily, and went to the fridge, he opened the door looked at the beer, closed the fridge door sat at the kitchen table and started weeping. It hadn't been long since Rita had left him, but he was missing her.

Chapter 9

George lifted his tea mug and clinked it against Jeff's, "you're looking a bit pissed off tonight, Jeff, what's up?"

Jeff quickly realising that he was not coming across as his normal self-replied, "Well, it all started when I received a call from the garage who informed me that my new Rolls Royce has a scratch on the paintwork, then I found out that the butler has run off with the new parlour maid, then, to top it all, don't you know, expressed with an over the top upper class accent, the gardener said that the fuchsias will not win first prize at the county show this year."

"Oh, what damnable luck dear chap," was George's reply using an even more accentuated upper-class accent.

Jeff, thinking thank God I have managed to get around that challenge, replies, lifting his tea mug, with his pinkie finger sticking out, "Yes, life can be so brutal sometimes, eh what."

Jock then joined in by asking, what he thought was a sensible question, "I didn't know you had a Rolls Jeff."

Jeff, looking at Jock in an understanding way and lifting the top of his recently purchased roll replied, "Only this Sweaty cheese one Jock."

"But I thought," Jock began to reply but Jeff was waving one of the evening news papers, that were on the table, in front of Jock's face in a cooling motion and added, "don't overheat Jock you've still got a night's work ahead of you, too many years of night trunking dulls your senses."

"No, it doesn't." Jock vigorously replied, "I could do that test thing that's in the paper to see if you could be a Computer Programmer, so I have applied for the training course."

"Oh shit, Jock, last week you wanted to be a Biologist because David Attenborough, up to his knees in bat shit, said there was a shortage of people who wanted to do the job, do you know what I think Jock, that you had better program your truck down the dock because the job you have got might slip away."

"No hurry they are all on strike down there with loads of pickets and I am no hero."

Finishing his tea George added, "I wonder what it's about this time."

Jeff felt more comfortable now as he was being included in the mundane banter that normally occurred before the night driving began.

"Talking of heroes," said Dave, "you know that bloke who always wears a white shirt and tie with the creases in his boiler suit trousers,"

"Yeah," was the combined reply from all at the table.

"Old Ted the toff," George added.

"Yeah, that's him," replied Dave, "well, he saw this woman trying to get a lift and he said she looked like she needed a favour so he pulled over and picked her up, well, it turned out this poor damsel in distress was a bloke and he pulled a knife on old Ted and made him drive up a country lane, where there were more of them, they dumped old Ted in a stinking ditch and drove off with his load."

"I am older than all of you and have been doing this job for more years, how many times have we talked about picking up women, you never know what will happen." They all agreed with Jeff, who they all considered like a father figure.

Jeff left the café and went to his Lorry thinking about Ted the toff being hijacked; unfortunately, the conversation with his daughter flooded his mind again.

He climbed into the cab and flicked open the work sheet and document folder for tonight's work trying hard to not to think of anything that had happened earlier.

Chapter 10

Paul had been to the apartment without Rita a couple of times for a week when he had a contract break and Rita was working and said she couldn't go with him and had not missed her as he felt now; he felt that it must be the finality of the situation. Then he thought should he have tried to contact her to try and make her change her mind. He knew that this thought really tested the amount he really loved her, was what she had said in her note, *not showing me love anymore* true, why had he not called her immediately after reading her note, why had he left it until after the project was completed successfully until he was having these feelings of emotion rather than anger and betrayal, did he really feel his work was more important than saving his marriage.

As Paul was turning this over in his mind a local friend, John, came through the side gate at the end of the drive.

"I could see you were in, your car is in the drive, but you didn't answer the door when I rang the bell," said John to Paul still sitting on the decking.

"Oh, hello mate," Paul replied.

"I see you are continuing where last night left off," John said looking at the empty beer bottles on the garden table.

"And why not when you have just finished a successful contract," Paul lied.

"Can I get you one John or is it too early for keep the village tidy supporters, you never know you might fall in someone's hedge if you over indulge again," John made a strangling motion with both his hands at Paul, "It really is a great place to live, this village, everybody reminds you of things that happened months and even years ago, yes I will now drink your beer, possibly great volumes to make up for the hurt you have created for me through that insensitive comment."

"Actually, John it's good to see you, I needed some company, pull up a pew," Paul replied as he got up and went to the fridge.

"Rita out on a retail therapy trip again then," John shouted in the direction of the rear door. Paul came back with two bottles of beer, "No not exactly," Paul paused, John noticed a change in the way Paul had said this and did not speak.

"I have shared things with you in the past and I know that with the gossips who live in this village that you are a mate I can trust," Paul confided.

"Shit Paul, what's up you sound too serious," added John.

"Well, I now realise it is serious, Rita has left me and gone to live with David," Paul said slowly giving John full eye contact.

"Oh, I knew they met for lunch in London every now and again, as wives of mates friends do sometimes, but I had no idea they had become that friendly, I'm sorry mate," John said consolingly.

"Well, that's something else I have just learnt about my wife, I had no idea that she met David, or anyone else I know, for lunch when she was at work."

John felt it time to change the subject and started to explain a yacht delivery trip that he had planned with an acquaintance called Peter who he had sailed with before. "This sounds interesting," said Paul.

Chapter 11

Jeff followed his usual route using all A roads that went through farmland rather than using a combination of A roads and motorway, which was shorter, but more prone to delays caused by breakdowns or accidents.

Along the section that is surrounded by acres of flat arable land, where there is limited number of trees, Jeff's headlights, on full beam, picked out the silhouette of what looked like a young girl hitching a lift. As he approached, hijacking raced through his thoughts combined with concern for the girl's safety at this time of night on a road that crossed open farmland.

As he approached the silhouette he slowed down, drawing closer he could see she had her arm outstretched with her thumb raised but was not looking over her shoulder as he approached. Jeff guessed that she could not be any taller than his granddaughter Lotti, which concerned him even more for her safety plus eliminating the thought that she may not be female.

He decided to pull over, in the lay-by a few yards ahead of where she was walking; thinking that if it was a trap that they would be unlucky as he was empty at this time in his shift.

The girl walked to below the open driver's window and looked up at Jeff. "Hi where are you going?" Jeff asked as he was taking a thorough look at her.

"I'm trying to get to St Catherine's," was her reply,

"Ok, I'm going that way, go round the front and climb up to the passenger's door."

As she passed in front of the headlights Jeff could see that she was simply a demure young girl, around the age of his granddaughter, his anxiety dissipated. Jeff's consternation for her safety returned as she climbed into the cab asking, "what is a young girl like you hitching a lift for anyway, I would have thought that you would have a boyfriend or a bunch of admirers breaking their necks to take you places,"

"That is a very nice thing to say, but no boyfriend no admirers just me, no commitments, nobody to be concerned about and nobody to be concerned about me, I am very grateful that you stopped for me though."

"Yes, I keep telling my younger driver workmates not to be tempted to pick up female passengers because they could pick up the wrong sort or something happens to her after you have dropped her off."

"I hope I don't get you into trouble," was her quiet reply.

The journey continued, with mainly Jeff talking, telling her about meeting his young workmates in the late-night café, Ted the Toff being hijacked, Jock and his job fantasies, which helped him keep his mind off his real issue; Rita leaving Paul and the effect it may have on his pregnant granddaughter Lottie.

There was a brief silence when the girl said, "You have so many stories maybe when you retire you should write a book to share them."

"Yes, I'm old but not that old yet, mind you, the years seem to have flown by since I turned fifty."

The girl, who was looking out of the side window turned her head slowly towards Jeff and added, "Yes, life is too short."

"I would like to know why you chose to be a Lorry driver."

Jeff started to explain that he didn't choose it that it chose him, realising that she had asked a very simple question that could be the basis of his direction in life.

He tried, delicately, to explain that he had made his girlfriend pregnant and felt the only way he could support a family was by driving. Starting with small vans that he could drive at nineteen years of age then eventually, passing his HGV 1 to earn more money as family expenses grew.

Jeff felt more comfortable telling stories about his early life at school rather than recent stories that continued to remind him of his daughter's and his wife's actions. He could hear himself telling an old school story that he hadn't told for a long time. "So, after all of us had stopped laughing he tried to carry on with the lesson and he started walking up and down between the desks when he noticed that one of the boy's textbooks was not covered in brown paper. He then walked to the front of the class and ordered the boy to join him at the front. The boy reluctantly stood up and joined the teacher at the front of the class. The teacher then said would you please enlighten me as to the reason for the absence of a cover on your textbook. The boy replied that he could not find any; the teacher's reply was, so your parents never receive any parcels. The boy replied no, the teacher said no what, the boy, whose timidity was now overtaking him, replied no parcels with a long pause then no sir rapidly following. Most of the class were crying with laughter because we knew that if we showed our humour we would be punished. The teacher continued, well then do your parents ever redecorate the rooms in your place of residence. Yes, sir was the immediate reply. Ah excellent, then we have a suitable material, was the teachers smug reply. As the teacher said now in a demonstrative voice, he grabbed the boy's tie and began to tie knots in it asking the boy what he was going to do when he arrived home this evening. The boy's reply was rapidly conveyed. I am going to cover my textbook with wallpaper sir. Good was the elongated teachers reply. The class could not contain their laughter any longer as we all felt that the teacher may not punish us as we were applauding his tie knotting. Taking the laughter as a signal of success the teacher added, you will not forget now will you. The boy looked down at his tie saying no sir, but my father is not going to be pleased sir. The teacher rapidly replied, "I am sure he will be able to spare a textbook size piece of old wallpaper." The boy looked at the teacher with despondency saying, no it is not that sir it is just that this is my father's best tie that he allowed me to wear today for doing well in the exam you last set for us."

The girl said, "I now know that you should write all of your stories to share them with other people and when you do write them down you can add just a short story about this young girl hitching a lift at night on her own, finishing her journey."

"Yes, you are right about finishing your journey as this is as far as I can get to St Catherine's."

"Many thanks," the girl replied gratefully. Jeff was very sad to see his passenger getting out of his cab and without forethought said, "For some reason I feel I have known you for ever, there are so many more stories I would like to share with you could we not try and meet again soon."

"I must finish my journey, I have enjoyed your company, I will never forget you and your kindness, but we will never be able to meet again, you are talented, but I do not think that you realise it. Will you promise me one thing, when you write your stories, write just a couple of lines about us meeting tonight so that it is never forgotten?" Before Jeff could say, that he would if he could the girl had left the cab and had disappeared from Jeff's sight into the darkness.

On the drive to the warehouse Jeff was immensely reflective on the calming effect that the girl passenger had on him. She appeared to have dissolved the negatives and guided him through the positives by asking simple questions then listening intently without any negative comments. As he arrived at the warehouse and reversed the lorry into the loading bay, he decided that she was different from anyone he had ever met, not from a loving relationship perspective, as she was young enough to be his granddaughter, but in that very short space of time she had had a profound effect on his motivation to improve his life by doing things that gave him pleasure and finding himself. He thought to himself how she did that! Then he said aloud, "oh shit is that what Rita is doing?"

Jeff asked one of the loading crew how long was it going to be until he was full, as he wanted to get an early start tonight.

"Oh, leave it out give us a chance what's the big rush tonight," was the abrasive reply.

"I don't want to waste anymore of my precious time," Jeff said, still thinking about what the young girl had said.

"Yes, being one of the oldest we can understand that, but just a reminder because you are an older person who has senior moments, you have been here less that ten minutes and if you think that we are going to work our balls off loading you quickly because you are wasting your precious time, do you know if we used bad language, we might tell you to fuck off but we are nice guys who don't use bad language." At this comment, from guys he had been working with for some time Jeff realised that he had had quite an eventful time over the past few hours and shouted sorry so that the loaders heard his reply over the noise of the forklift trucks.

He thanked the loading crew before leaving, as he felt they did load him quicker tonight. He turned on the radio following his usual routine on this very unusual day he thought as he pressed the radio button. The radio was tuned into the local radio station that broadcast local traffic news which in the past Jeff had found very useful. Because he had left the depot a little earlier the local news was still being broadcast Jeff listened vaguely. His attention to the broadcast sharpened when he heard the newsreader describing the young girl that he had picked up. "Local Police would like to speak to anyone who feels they know this person from the description we have given." Jeff shuddered wishing he had paid more attention to the beginning of the news broadcast. What had happened to her after he had dropped her off raced through his mind, followed by thoughts of where was the nearest Police Station Jeff, still shocked from what he had heard, then realised that there was a large Police Station on the dual carriageway he was using at that moment, and he knew he could park the lorry easily.

Jeff enters the Police Station through the main entrance. There is a wooden counter directly in front of him and behind it was a Police Sergeant talking on a telephone. The Sergeant nod at Jeff and with his free arm indicates that Jeff should take a seat. As Jeff turns to sit, he realises that there is a woman of about forty years of age already sitting, making his way to a spare seat opposite the woman he suddenly realises that he should be making deliveries and what would be his excuse for being late as he had left early plus, he felt that he could not tell the bosses the real reason for going to the Police Station as he should not have stopped to pick up a passenger. Where had all those positive feelings gone, what had happened to the young girl who had given him such positive feelings on such a negative day caused by his daughter Rita, and he had no idea that because of Rita's actions that he would be seeing the inside of another police station sooner than he expected.

"Silly cow," was the unexpected declaration from the woman sitting opposite. Jeff stopped looking at his hands as he clicked his thumbnails and looked across at the woman.

"He's shacked up somewhere, probably getting what she won't give him at home, bloody ask for it don't they."

As the woman was looking directly at Jeff, he assumed she had begun a conversation and his instant reply was "sorry."

"Her on the telephone."

"Sorry I wasn't listening," Jeff replied putting his face into his hands. "You OK dear?" said the woman now looking concerned.

"Yeah," said Jeff quietly.

"You haven't had an accident, or something have you,"

"No not an accident," was Jeff's laboured reply.

"Well dear if you ask me, you don't look so happy about something," the woman replied as she walked across the reception room and grabbed Jeff's hand, "Christ love, you're shaking, I'd better get that copper quick."

"No," was Jeff's abrupt reply.

"But what have you,"

"Nothing," Jeff interrupted, "I don't think I want to hear what they have got to say," Jeff paused, "I think they'll say she's dead."

"Oh Jesus," the woman said quietly realising her incapability to deal with the problem. She then noticed that the Policeman had finished the telephone call and went over and asked him if he could see the man sitting down over there, pointing to Jeff, "he's shaking and talking about a dead woman." The Policeman looked over at Jeff and nodded in agreement with the woman. He then walked from the back of the counter, put his hand on Jeff's shoulder and said, "Let's use the interview room sir and you can tell me why you have come to the station tonight." Jeff stood slowly and followed the policeman.

"Now tell me about it," was the Policeman's opening comment.

"On local radio you said that if anyone can give information about a young girl, I know I should not have done it whilst working but she looked so vulnerably hitching on that dark road and she didn't look much older than my granddaughter."

"OK sir, I now know what you are referring to. A young girl's body has been found."

"Oh, shit she's dead," Jeff said, lowering his face into his hands.

The Police Sergeant asked Jeff to give him all the details about picking up the girl hitchhiker and when Jeff had finished, he left the interview room after telling Jeff that he needed to look at the information on the case in the main office.

Jeff sat in the room feeling sick and lightheaded for what seemed like forever, the interview room door reopened Jeff looked at the Sergeants face immediately, and the Sergeant returned the glance with a wistful half smile. "I am sorry that you have been troubled Sir, the young girl's body was found over twenty-four hours ago, and the forensic pathologist's report says that she had been dead for a number of hours, so your hitchhiker must have been another young female, and may I suggest that you do not give hitchhikers lifts in the future."

Jeff continued to look the Sergeant directly in the face, "but the description on the radio was identical," Jeff muttered quietly.

"Thank you for coming into the station sir you may leave now," the Sergeant replied concerned at the reaction Jeff had to what he felt was good news.

" Yes OK, I am going now, sorry to have bothered you."

Jeff began to open the door to the interview room and turned to the Sergeant unexpectantly. "Can you tell me where the young girl's body was discovered?"

"Yes sir, it was part of the radio broadcast, she was found on Farm Road on the route leading to St Catherine's."

"Oh shit, that's where I picked her up."

"Yes, sir I realised that when you were giving me the details, and as we have agreed the girl who you gave an illegal lift to was not our girl, I advise you to be on your way, and please do not stop for any other hitchhikers." He climbed back into his truck thinking, today has been weird, Rita has left Paul and now I think that I 've given a lift to a young female ghost. God I am getting old. As Jeff started the engine, he looked across at the passenger seat and remembered her parting comments that they would never be able to meet again as she had to finish her journey, he needed to write a story that mentioned picking her up, so it would never be forgotten.

At the end of his night shift Jeff felt that he must call Paul. Jeff started the conversation by telling Paul about his strange night, feeling concerned about Rita's actions, but eventually he told Paul that she had called him and told him about David. Paul could not hold back and said, "thanks for calling Jeff, I would like to kill the bastard." As Jeff put the phone down, he exclaimed loudly again, "oh shit what a night."

Chapter 12

David was very satisfied when he received the phone call from Rita on Saturday evening telling him that she was leaving Paul the following day and that she would be at his house sometime on Sunday.

He realised that there had been good news and bad news that week, Rita moving in was good news, with her fantastic body. The bad news had been the questions from the auditors at work asking why he had done so much business with the company called Phoenix.

After the call he poured himself a glass of scotch and sat in the lounge. He began to think about her, but he could not prevent himself from thinking, why it had taken her so long to make up her mind to leave her husband. His thoughts wandered back to when he was in his early teens when girls at school tried to side-track him into agreeing to take them out, mainly to the local picture house where they would sit as close as possible and try to get him to kiss them. He remembered that the girls that his other classmates, at the time, considered to be the prettiest girls, chatted to him and were always around him in the playground and other places he went. He realised at this time, in early teens, that girls thought that he was good looking. As time passed, he began to use this female attraction to his advantage. He remembered how he had found juggling with female attention and studying for exams a bit of a struggle as he had always had the drive to get a well-paid job and realised early that he needed to get good grades in school exams.

As he took a large swig of his drink, he nodded thinking that was a long time ago, your first wife even left you for another man, so she could not have thought that you were that good looking, but Rita must think you are, as she is leaving Paul to be with you.

He took another swig of his drink nodding again thinking how he could steer the auditors away from Phoenix. He realised that he needed to reduce the Phoenix credit balance as soon as possible just in case the auditors had ways of finding out bank account details. He needed to transfer money to the account that he had setup in Rita's name he felt that this would be a good account to use as now she would be living with him that it would be easier to get her to sign things without knowing what it was that she was signing. She had started to ask more detailed questions about the security sign in system at his office that he had used a few times.

Rita, being the wife of his friend Paul, had been useful as a working relationship in the early days of Phoenix but now being more physical and committed, plus Rita moving in, he suddenly realised had complications as well as advantages. He nodded at the glass in his hand, thinking, we have fixed things up to now so just continue to fix things in the future, he told himself. "Oh shit," he said out loud as he remembered that he had decided to buy Rita a welcome present. He decided that he had not drunk enough to stop him driving so he put the unfinished glass on the kitchen table as he picked up his car keys.

The mobile phone shop was very helpful. They had sold him a smart phone with an immediate O2 contract and had given him the new number. He hoped that she would never give anyone else this number this would be just for them to talk.

He managed to park easily at the Peugeot showroom. He entered through the automatic opening doors and did not see the three young sales attendants who looked over, who then looked at each other.

In prime position in the showroom was the model that he had been considering for Rita. He felt that she would like a convertible for good weather with a solid roof for winter weather. He opened the driver's door and sat in the leather driver's seat thinking that Rita is sure to appreciate the smell of the leather interior as she had already shown him how nice smells affected her.

One of the sales attendants had approached and was standing at the side of the car. "Can I help you Sir?" he said as he lowered himself to look at his potential customer.

"I like this one," was David's instant reply.

"yes, it is a very sort after model Sir due to the hard reclining roof."

"Can you deliver this particular car this afternoon?" David's reply obviously shocked the attendant as all he could reply was "eeeer."

"I will organise a bank draft now as long as you guarantee that this particular car will be at the address, I give you this afternoon."

"I am sure that we can achieve your request Sir, but I just need to check with my manager."

"Ok, please be quick as I am busy today." The Sales Attendant walked towards the desk, and his two colleagues, feeling very dazed by David's unusual request but overwhelmed by the thought that he had never earned his sales commission so rapidly before. "Another time waster?" one of his colleagues said as he approached.

Chapter 13

John was surprised that Paul had agreed to the trip so quickly, especially as it was only a couple of days after he had mentioned it. John called Peter immediately after their chat and Peter said was it was good as it helped with the watch routine.

Paul and John arrived at 3pm in Cowes, Isle of Wight on the Red Jet ferry from Southampton. Paul had enjoyed the train journey from their village; he wondered why he had never used the train service when he was contracting for his customers. He then realised it was because the speed of life he had to maintain needed the convenience of a car. A lifestyle, he now knew, he was trying to change. He realised he did not need to support Rita's needs anymore, only his own. Little did he know what the future held.

John had told Paul that they would be meeting the delivery skipper, Peter, at the Anchor pub at 4pm. During the train journey John had been recounting some of the stories Peter had told him when they had first met at John's yacht club; Paul realised that Peter had been delivering yachts for several years so a trip to Portugal didn't seem too daunting. They both agreed that they were in good time and that they had planned it well so far. "Let's hope that the rest of the voyage goes to plan for us and your mate Peter," Paul added sarcastically.

Peter was at the pub when they arrived, and he took over the planning discussion. Paul simply sat listening, thinking how relaxing it was not to oversee events for once in his life. His mind briefly touched on the Sunday when Rita had told him she was leaving, as he was checking his project implementation plans, he shivered as he suddenly felt that was his previous life, this being the first time he had ever considered it in that way. He then shook his head slightly as if the thought had been a fly settling on his head that he must get rid of and decided he must listen to Peter and his plan for the trip down the Bay of Biscay to Portugal.

The immediate plan, set that night, was to buy and load provisions on board the following day so much of the discussion was about what anyone disliked eating, Peter soon realised that John and Paul were a couple of gastronomic dustbins which pleased him. Peter also stated that it was necessary to take the yacht out for a 'shake down' sail in the Solent so that John and Paul could become familiar with the deck and rigging layout of 'Obsession' a 38-foot cruising yacht. Peter also informed them that he had started to chart a course from Cowes, given the current weather pattern, leaving an hour before high water on Sunday. John and Paul felt comfortable with all Peter's plans. John and Paul had sailed together before, but many months ago, when Paul was between customer contracts. Both knew that all yachts had their own idiosyncrasies, Paul felt that was why yachts were called She, which you needed to be in tune with especially in rough weather, which Paul had experienced with his own She. Neither of them had sailed across the Bay of Biscay and like everyone else they had heard how rough it could become. John had reassured Paul that he could trust Peter's judgment, particularly regarding weather patterns and their interpretation, as Peter has been delivering yachts for many years and had thousands of ocean sea mile experience. Paul took John's word for it, feeling a deeper thought that he had been let down by other people too much recently, God could not be that cruel, again, could he?

Paul had called Lottie before agreeing with John to make the trip as he was concerned that her baby, his grandchild, was due. In September. He was very pleased when Lottie said that he should go and enjoy himself as it was a while yet before his grandchild was due. She added that she was sad that her parents had separated but that life must go on, and that how much they both hated David for taking her mother away and those sorts of friends should not exist.

Chapter 14

On the way home to inner London after viewing the two properties the car buzzed with the discussion between Lottie and Kevin. The main facilities and accommodation in both properties were very similar and they both agreed that they were more than adequate. However, Kevin was bias towards the property on the outskirts of Redford, mainly because he could walk to the main line station. Lottie was bias towards the property in Amberton, as she felt very comfortable inside the house and with the village. The feeling of peace had always been very important to Lottie, even more now with her recent news about her mother and father's separation.

Kevin listened carefully to how Lottie described their future in the village and soon realising that he would be at work and out of the village for much more time than Lottie, he decided that Amberton was the place to be with Lottie to raise a happy family.

They agreed that they would need to make an offer as soon as they arrived home. They had discovered that the property in Amberton was vacant possession because the owner, an elderly lady, was now living in a care home and had decided that she was happier living there than she would be if she returned to her house in Amberton. In the care home she had made friends with so many people who had so many stories to share.

The situation with the property owner worried Kevin. When the Manager of the estate agent had shown them around all the furniture was still in place. Lottie had found this comforting and stabilising, it felt like a real home. Lottie had asked the manager if the care home was far away. When he said that it was just outside Redford Lottie could not help saying that if they went ahead with the purchase could the owner be contacted or visited. The manager explained that he was dealing with her son and daughter and that he would ask them.

As they got closer to inner London Kevin's worrying increased, his brain was spinning with all the plans. His job as a Project Planner at work had taken over. He realised that there were critical issues, selling their apartment, agreeing a mortgage, getting a survey, their offer being realistic and being accepted. But above all, timing, their child was due in September. Would the baby arrive early or late? Would they move before or after the birth? How would this affect the hospital Lottie had chosen? Kevin became more tense and anxious.

"Kevin," said Lottie, "you don't seem as happy as I am that we have found our future family home, why?"

Kevin started to list all the issues he had been thinking about.

"Yes darling, that's making plans which will be fun, but we should be happy making the plans not stressed."

"But what if things don't go to our plan?"

"Then they were not meant to go to our plan and another plan will be there for us to consider, you may laugh but this is how I am guided, this is how I have come to terms that my mother and father are not a unit anymore."

"Oh," said Kevin's disbelievingly.

"Do you have faith in yourself," quizzed Lottie.

"More now that I have been promoted,"

"No not just at work,"

"Well work is a significant part of my life," added Kevin.

"Yes, I know darling, but I am now talking about inner strength, the inner strength that I love you for, how you are a really caring person, not just for me and our new family, but when we discuss things that are happening around us and in other parts of the world you genuinely care."

" Well," Kevin said quizzically.

Lottie thought hard before she replied. "Well, I believe that I am cared for by my guide that you find so funny."

Kevin paused before answering. "I think that you either have an overflow of inner strength, or things have always gone right for you." At that moment Kevin parked the car in their normal parking space at home.

As they walked to their apartment, they bumped into their neighbour Roddy, an American who had lived next door for about six months. Caring Lottie commented on how tired she felt he looked as she said hello.

"Yes, I have been in the office all day," Roddy replied slowly and wearily, "the American money market is taking a great deal of my time lately, in fact one of the Vice Presidents is due here in four weeks' time on a long term stay to help out."

"Well, don't wear yourself out before he gets here," Lottie added as she placed her hand on his shoulder.

"Enough about me, how's the mother carrying my new neighbour."

"We are spiffing don't you know?" Lottie said with an upper-class accent.

"That's why I really like you as neighbours you are so top hole," Roddy replied with his best British accent.

"But that is now due to change," Kevin added.

"Today we have found a village and a house that we both like," Lottie said, as she looked Kevin in the eyes.

"Yes, but now we must sell our apartment," Kevin returned Lottie's eye contact.

"Right," said Roddy thoughtfully as he put the key into his front door lock. "I am really going to miss you two, sorry three," he added.

Sipping tea together Lottie and Kevin made a list of things to be done. There was a knock at their apartment door. "I'm not expecting anyone, are you darling," Kevin asked Lottie as he went to the door. Lottie shook her head as she could hear "Hi again man, I have a proposition," Roddy said excitedly.

Roddy explained that his company owns his apartment as it is cheaper and better than staying in hotels and with the Vice President coming for a long stay, they would like to buy theirs as well. He had just called the President of the company and he was allowed to negotiate and then the President would need to agree the price. "So, let's negotiate Kevin," Roddy said as he slapped Kevin on the back. "Well, I will get you both a beer," Lottie said with a massive smile.

The price was fixed and agreed with the President plus a completion date of end of August. Roddy had said that in the USA they normally buy property within two weeks, but four weeks is fine. Kevin and Lottie tried to withhold their excitement but failed, Kevin and Roddy sealed the verbal deal with a glass of malt whiskey, a bottle Kevin had been saving for a special occasion.

The move went exactly to plan. Lottie sent her mother and father a text to tell them her news. Paul replied and congratulated them. Rita did not reply which worried Lottie, she tried to call but there was no answer.

During August everything went to the plan that Lottie and Kevin had put together. Payment for the apartment from Roddy's company was paid to their solicitor the morning of the date set for the move. Lottie had slowly packed their loose things like clothes and cooking equipment, as their baby was now due in two weeks' time.

Kevin and Lottie sat on their three-piece suit in the living room in their new house holding hands and looking each other in the eyes. "Your guide has been with us all month," Kevin said as he gently touched Lottie's cheek. "No Kevin our guide is with us all the time," Lottie gently contradicted him. "Ahh…" Lottie let go of Kevin's hand and clutched her stomach. "Kevin, I think the saying is true, new home…….new baby."

Chapter 15

During the 'shake down' sail, which had gone well for Paul and John, even a small compliment from Peter, the wind died. Peter decided to motor sail back to the marina. A short distance from the marina the diesel inboard spluttered and came to a halt. Peter shouted "no problem we have a soft breeze in the right direction so we will make the visitors' berth OK," Paul was able to witness, first-hand; the way Peter controlled an unexpected situation. He also witnessed the skill he had controlling the yacht and his effective communication with his new crew. No aggression, just short simple instructions in perfect time. Paul realised that when unexpected things happened during his project work and his life with Rita in general that he hadn't been anyway near as calm and collected. Also, that Rita had usually been the one that had taken the brunt of his anger. He suddenly felt ashamed. He shivered again as he realised, he must try to concentrate on controlling his emotions when stressed.

Peter left the boat quickly, as Paul and John were making her fast in the visitor's berth, heading for the marina office. He returned a while later and said, "it's all sorted, 'Obsession' is being hauled out later today, depending on what they find we will make a plan, now it's Anchor time, so who's buying?" Paul was slightly shocked realising that Peter soon disregarded obstacles and got on with enjoying his life, another lesson, Paul thought, that he had learnt that day.

"I don't know if John has told you, but I run a dry boat," Peter said calmly as Paul brought the drinks to the table in the corner of the Anchor.

"Well, I hoped I wouldn't need to swim," Paul replied quickly without considering the statement.

"Well as I can't swim, I guess my dry boat rule has a double whammy," Peter replied with a joking teacher like action with his finger at Paul and John.

"Sorry Paul I forgot," John interrupted, "Peter's rule is that nobody drinks alcohol when at sea,"

"Excellent rule," Paul added quickly again without considering how he had been relying on visits to the local pub back home since Rita's departure. As he moved the chair to sit at the table, he felt that this was probably a blessing in disguise, he knew he needed to control his drinking, he also knew that it had started to become his emotional prop. He raised his eyes to the ceiling of the pub and mentally thanked God for looking after him. "So, when ashore we make the most of it," Peter added looking at the barmaid, "so you had better go and get another round in quickly John, as our gorgeous barmaid is not serving right now,"

"Alright skipper," John said as he stood and made a fake salute, "I realise that one didn't touch your throat on its way down,"

"Boson you should know that by now, especially after a long ocean crossing."

Feeling more relaxed than he had felt for a long while in Peter's easy-going company, Paul suddenly realised that he was looking over the top of his glass as he drunk at the barmaid. Another masculine trait, he thought, that I have not been doing for some years. He began to feel embarrassed with himself as his subconscious was imagining the feel of her body, against his, in a romantic embrace. He could hear his conscious brain telling him to stop. But he felt better aligning with his subconscious as she was very attractive, and he was virtually single. "After the next pint we need to go back to the boatyard they should have 'Obsession' out of the water by now," Peter said stroking his stubble from side to side with his left hand which was as rough, and weather beaten and made a noise like strong wind blowing through yacht rigging.

"What do you think has happened, could it be a replacement engine?" asked Paul, grateful that his attention to the barmaid's flowing lines and graceful movements had been interrupted.

"It's a new engine only been used for a few hours, according to the owner, reckon we've picked something up round the prop shaft, the Solent is full of crap these days, it's a pig, because the weather pattern on the isobar chart is good for a Biscay crossing right now."

"Reading weather patterns is something I'd like to understand better," Paul added to Peter's remorse statement, feeling that he had obviously been rubbish at reading the weather pattern of his own life.

"We can share the isometric lows and highs on this trip, and here comes another high," Peter laughed as John arrived with the next round of drinks.

Paul reflected as John placed the glasses on the small table because he hadn't read Rita's lows and highs more accurately, how selfish he felt he had been.

Paul had spent as much time as he could in the Anchor waiting for the repairs on 'Obsession' to be finished. He had discovered, to his initial dismay, that the barmaid, Sindy, had a female partner. Slowly coming to terms with this surprise, whilst continuing discussion, he found her easier to talk to than friends, either male or female, that he had known for many years. Sindy had planted a significant seed in Paul's barren field that every romantic partner needs to be shown that they are loved. Not just financial support but in simple natural ways, listening, touching, and trying to share their lows and highs. A seed that Paul would discover grew well in the weeks that followed.

Chapter 16

Rita realised that her early days with David were wonderful, his attention, his caring, his generosity, especially when he had bought her a new car and mobile phone that were there when she arrived at his home.

But now she was concerned. Where was all this money coming from. Apart from the car and phone he was continuously putting £100 in her handbag plus continuously eating out in what she knew were expensive restaurants. She enjoyed being pampered but she realised she had no idea where the money was coming from, unlike her marriage to Paul where they had a joint bank account, and she knew when he was paid for a contract. She remembered the chat she had with Sue, a shiver went down her spine, she now knew that, apart from physically, she knew nothing of David's life when he was not with her. She felt she needed to know more.

Chapter 17

The trip started on Tuesday, from Cowes to the Needles, providing Paul with an unforgettable memory, 'Obsession' had a music system with waterproof speakers in the cockpit and Peter played his CDs of Mary Black. Paul found the words of the songs and her voice haunting and thought stimulating. Why had he never been introduced to this type of music before? His thoughts took over. In your other life real things happening like this, were too easily overlooked.

Peter had devised a two-hour watch system, which he was keeping an eye on during the first day also making sure that John and Paul were competent and comfortable with the arrangement. Paul handed over watch to John at two o'clock that afternoon and Paul asked Peter about their course and where the next waypoint was. Peter was concentrating on the weather charts and simply answered Bayonna, Paul realised that he needed the sea chart to understand better.

Paul sat in the cockpit of Obsession in Villa Mora marina. He had found the soft padded cockpit cushions, something that had not been used on their trip so far.

They had arrived at 4.30am that morning and had pulled into the visitor's berth and then immediately turned into their bunks. Paul and John had both woken just before nine o'clock that morning. After a morning coffee they both realised that the two-hour watch system that Peter had made them all follow had changed their sleeping pattern. Peter was still asleep, they both agreed that he was probably more used to his own system. They also agreed to follow Peter's other system and take him a mug of coffee, remembering Peter's instruction, that whenever you relieved Peter on watch the person relieving him must take him a coffee.

Unfortunately, when Paul and John arrived at Peter's bunk, with the coffee, he was awake. Peter's remark being, "so which one of you two is on watch now then." Peter's humour had been a real blessing during the trip, particularly crossing the Bay of Biscay with the wind blowing a force six both Paul and John had mentioned the wave size to Peter, he had replied, "no wind, no waves, I know which I would not like to lose in a sailing yacht."

After the morning coffee Peter told Paul and John that he needed to register the boat and crew with the Marina and Portuguese authorities. To do this he needed everyone's passport. John decided to accompany Peter, as he would like to witness the way the authorities dealt with yachts that simply arrive early morning. Paul was also interested but decided that he needed another cup of coffee to help him wake up before mentally dealing with a formal situation. Peter described his lack of mental capacity as 'land sickness' and made him stand on the solid jetty and remain still. As Peter and John started to laugh Paul realised that he was moving to compensate for the motion of the yacht on which he was no longer standing. Peter added that 'land sickness' not only affects your physical stability but also your mental stability and as he felt that Paul must have been mentally unstable to accept this trip in England, he needed to keep away from the authorities so that

Peter and John could formally register now they were in Portugal. Another piece of Peter humour, Paul realised but was quite happy to obey Peter's inference as he needed a little time alone to gather his thoughts as so many lives changing events had happened during the past month.

Paul realised that the soft cushions were quite comfortable as he finished his last mouthful of coffee. From his comfy seat he stretched to look around the marina wondering into which free berth Obsession would be going and whilst doing so he spotted Peter and John leaving the marina office. He noticed that they had only walked a few paces when Peter was embraced by a female, who from the distance of the visitor's berth looked quite attractive to Paul.

Paul continued to watch Peter and John as they walked back to Obsession and as they boarded Paul could not resist saying to Peter, "one in every port skipper,"

"Yes, and that is where I have learnt to leave them," Peter replied jokingly and abruptly. Realising that he may have briefly lifted the lid on one of Peter's cans of worms Paul changed the subject.

"So, we are all now formally visitors in Portugal?"

"Yep," John replied, "but Peter was treated by them in the office like he is a returning resident."

"Well, I have been here quite a few times," Peter added.

"Plus, we have been invited to dinner with Peter's Portuguese friends tonight. Are these male or female friends?" Paul asked seriously but with a smile.

"Well, you had better come and find out," was Peter's terse reply, adding, "but I advise you both to go to the marina shower block before we eat as we all smell of the Bay of

Biscay and my Portuguese friends will find that will hinder them eating the food that you two will be buying them."

"Oh, so dinner is on us tonight then?" John asked light heartedly. "Yep, been my routine for many visits now, but seeing that you two are both earning far more than I will ever earn delivering other people's big toys you two can foot the bill for both dinner and what usually follows after a dry crossing of the Bay."

"Oh, a piss up," Paul and John said almost simultaneously.

"Where we go, they only take cash so you may need to use the Plastic Bank machine, which is up near the marina office, John, you saw it didn't you."

"Yes skipper," John replied to giving Peter a drawn-out salute.

"But before you both disappear to the cash machine; we need to put Obsession in her allocated berth."

"Yes skipper," Paul replied copying John's salute.

Paul and John found the cash machine and John was surprised when his card was entered that he could choose the language he could use to make the transaction happen, turning to Paul saying, "You didn't have anything to do with this system did you?"

"No unfortunately."

"I thought not, it works too well."

"There is one thing I like about you John," Paul replied with his mid finger of his right hand raised with the other fingers pressed into his palm by his thumb.

"Why, you are so kind, there are two things I like about you," John replied raising two fingers of his right hand, with a laugh.

Using the cash machine so far from home by simply entering his pin number made John think about cash fraud as Paul was using the machine. "You look very pensive," was Paul's comment as he replaced his card and secured the money in his pocket.

"I was just thinking how easy these machines are for criminals to take your money anywhere in the world, steal a British card and pin and go abroad, how do our British authorities keep control of theft like this."

"With difficulty I would imagine," Paul said slowly stroking his unshaven stubble with his hand.

"The only thing that uniquely identifies anybody is their fingerprints, so why haven't machines like these been upgraded to recognize fingerprints, you have been in technology for most of your life, why haven't you done it?" John light heartedly said as he jabbed Paul's arm with his pointed finger.

"No, since Rita buggered off with Dave, I don't work in IT anymore, no need. I think I will start doing yacht delivery with Peter; you meet better people, apart from crew members like you of course."

When they arrived back at Obsession, Peter asked them both if either of them had a mobile phone, "I need to call the owner and tell him that Obsession is here and what berth she is in, and I don't want to walk to a pay phone."

"I brought mine and a charger, but I haven't switched it on since leaving Cowes so when I do switch it on, I need to let outstanding messages come through before you can use it. I will get it from my bag," Paul explained to Peter.

"Thanks Paul."

Paul came up from below with his phone. "No real messages to be concerned about," he said but deep down wishing that Rita had tried to contact him. Peter dialled the owner's number and told him the berth number, the owner said that he would try and book the earliest flight maybe tomorrow or the next day if this did not cause Peter and his crew any problems. "Oh well guys only tonight and then we must leave Obsession free for the owner, good life yacht delivery eh, still tonight we will privately celebrate our arrival."

Paul and John headed for the shower block armed with what toiletries they had brought plus what they considered to be their smartest looking clothes. The shower cubicles looked inviting thought Paul entering the first one that had the door open. He soon realised that John had occupied the one adjacent when he started singing "Oh what a beautiful morning oh what a beautiful day," the words made him smile. He started by washing his hair which, like the rest of his body, had not been washed since he left home some eight or nine days earlier. My god he thought how many days it has been I am usually so meticulous about time keeping and timing generally. No, he continued to think, that was my previous life in IT. As he continued to wash, his mind was in free fall, before the trip, the trip itself, particularly when at the end of the Bay of Biscay the yacht was surrounded by several dolphins that swam alongside for a couple of hours, they were so graceful. He closed his eyes as he showered his face and was able to mentally visualize the dolphins gracefully swimming alongside. Suddenly he turned his face away from the shower and said in a loud voice "Shit I could do that."

John stopped singing, "What deliver yachts full time," he replied. John's voice from the next cubicle surprised Paul as he realised that he had been away in his own thoughts. "No mate, I will tell you later, it is about the fingerprint question that you chided me about earlier."

They both walked back to the yacht after using all the deodorants and after shave dispensers they had brought. "John, I think we both probably smell like a Chinese brothel."

"Yes, I agree but who knows Peter's Portuguese female friends may find our smell and our Bay of Biscay tan a real turn on."

"I will not tell Sandy you said that when we get back home."

"Great, but I was really thinking of you Paul not me."

This was the first time John had really raised the issue regarding Paul's separation since the chat they had had in Paul's Garden on the day Paul had quickly decided to join him on the delivery trip. "Good, but I think I will adopt Peter's principle when I start doing deliveries, yes one in every port but I will also leave them there," laughing loudly John added, "I wonder what Portuguese brothels smell like, maybe Peter has that planned after we get pissed maybe that is what he really meant by leaving them there," "Peter is a bright bloke but having sailed with him now I do not think that subtly is one of his best attributes," "never mind at least we smell right and look sort of right."

Peter returned from the shower block, Paul and John were sitting in the cockpit discussing how hungry they felt and wondering what might be on the menu tonight, but both stopped talking when they looked at Peter's attire.

"Shit mate you make us two look like we are in working men's clothes."

"Well, you didn't ask me about what clothes to bring so I didn't need to tell you that we always dress for dinner on our first day after arriving."

"Yes, very subtle," replied John looking at Paul and winking.

"Ok let's go to my local, the bar where I usually meet my friends on arrival," Peter said to John and Paul as he climbed over the stanchions and on to the jetty.

"Aye skipper," they both said as they joined Peter on the jetty, which rocked a little with their additional weight.

"Steady crew we haven't even had our first drink yet and you are both unbalanced."

"Sorry skipper," John said holding onto Obsession's guardrail as he did his mock salute with his other hand.

" Actually, I have just made a serious error. You two are no longer crew, you are now a pair of bankers."

"Sorry skipper, the wind blowing through the rigging prevented me from hearing that correctly. If I heard you correctly, does this mean that you are not going to introduce Paul and I to your friends when we get to the bar?"

"Bankers is what I said," Peter shouted.

He was heard by people, obviously English speaking, who were busy on the decks of their yachts, one of whom replied as they passed his berth, "Yes we get loads of them here who think they can sail a yacht." Peter, realising he was losing the plot continued to walk purposefully along the main jetty towards the gang planking that extended up to the marina banking. John and Paul walked at the same speed as Peter but a couple of paces behind as John had asked Paul about the statement that he shouted when they were in the shower. Paul was explaining to John that his idea was about owners of mobile phones being able to record their finger print on touch screen iPhone to prevent any other person being able to use it if the phone was lost or stolen and that when he shouted "I can do that," in the shower it was because he had worked out, in his mind, how he could write the program code to perform this type of app, but just as John was about to ask Paul more about the way this app would work they followed Peter into a bar where there was at least a dozen people, both men and women, who greeted Peter giving him a large glass of beer and telling him that it had only just been poured as they saw him walking up the pathway towards the bar, they all knew that Peter preferred his beer freshly poured and chilled. Paul told John that he would tell him more about his idea later. They both decided to buy themselves a drink as Peter and his friends were having several ebullient conversations and they both agreed that Peter was not going to formally introduce them.

"Well, we made it," John said to Paul as they both clinked their large glasses of beer.

"Yep, and I haven't felt more alive since I don't know when, thanks to your suggestion that I join you, so a real thanks mate," Paul said clinking John's glass a second time.

"What's more you seem to have thought of a new business idea as well," John added before taking another long slurp of his beer.

"I could seriously get used to drinking this beer."

"Yes, me too, a long break from drinking has made me appreciate it more," Paul added thinking that his break from Rita had had the same effect.

"Tell me seriously John have you ever seen a mobile phone ad that includes fingerprint security."

"No mate, that was what immediately came to mind when you mentioned the idea earlier and to be honest, I have no idea why somebody hasn't thought of it."

"No, me neither, let's ask Peter's friends, if we ever get chatting to them, if they have ever heard of a mobile phone company that offers this function."

"Yes, I have heard British accents as well as Portuguese accents speaking broken English, Peter seems to have a real mix of friends," John said as he looked around for somebody, they could introduce themselves to. He stopped looking when he saw two women sitting at a table towards the rear of the small bar. John felt that they looked a similar age, if not a little younger, to Paul and himself.

"Let's go and introduce ourselves to those two women Paul."

"They don't look like they are joining in with the rest of Peter's crowd," Paul replied as they both forced themselves past some Portuguese females who were engaging Peter in very broken English conversation. Peter nodded as they passed. John and Paul both assumed that Peter did not wish to interrupt the broken English conversation the attractive Portuguese woman was trying to have with him.

"Bon Dia, Ola," John said to the two women as he approached with his hand outstretched expecting either of them to reciprocate and shake his hand. It did not happen. Instead, the woman with short but fashionable fair hair said, "No speaky Portuguese."

"Oh, thank God for that because all I can say is hello good day I no speaky either." The fair-haired woman pointing at her friend with equally fashionably styled brunette hair said, "So we look Portuguese rather than English. I am not sure whether we should consider that a compliment or not."

"I think we should take it as a compliment," her friend added looking around the bar.

"The English word that comes to mind for, what I believe to be Portuguese girls, in this bar, is Stunning."

"Yes, Peter does appear to have some attractive friends, how long have you two known him."

"Well, I think we have just been given a further compliment," the fair-haired woman said to her friend slanting her head towards John. "But the problem we have continuing this conversation is that we have no idea who this Peter is."

"Oh, so you are not here to celebrate our, or should I say Peter's, arrival."

"No, we are here to celebrate our own arrival, well to be more accurate, to have our first drink for over a week, so you two and the mysterious Peter have only recently arrived as well?"

Simultaneously John and Paul answered, "Yes."

"Well, it appears we have at least one subject in common that we can discuss with these two men, who have not formally introduced themselves, who have just interrupted our private conversation," the fair-haired woman shared with her friend with a broad smile.

John and Paul shared a brief glance at each other ending with John nodding his head at Paul and indicating with a sideways motion to the two women that Paul was elected to tell them their names. "I'm Paul and this is John along with Peter who is that guy over there talking to those two women,"

Paul said pointing and looking at the two for a sign of recognition, "we have delivered a yacht to this marina from Cowes, you are now at an advantage over us as we do not know your names and I do understand that your names could easily be Ms Piss-Off and Ms Leave-us-alone John and I would be disappointed, but we would leave you to your private conversation."

Well, you are both invited to stay for the simple reason that I have never heard such an interesting introduction before."

"No neither have I," agreed John "and we have just shared the Bay of Biscay with each other," John paused looking at Paul, "and our glasses are nearly empty so can we go one stage further and offer you two a drink."

"Yes, you can buy Brenda and me a good bottle of dry white wine," was the reply from the one with fair hair. "Certainly, but is 'me' short for a name, as I have never heard it before," John replied with a sheepish grin.

"Yes, I can tell you've spent time crossing the Bay as your ability to communicate on dry land has slipped overboard, 'me' is short for Barbara. So, while your friend is buying the drinks Paul, you can tell Brenda and me, oh sorry using the short version, Barbara, how many yachts you three deliver and to where you deliver them."

Paul explained that this was his first delivery with Peter and how the trip had been arranged, carefully leaving out the reason he was sitting in his back garden drinking beer, by telling them that he ran his own business and that a weighty contract had just been completed with nothing of any importance planned as a follow on, adding that at the time he needed a break. "So, you found that sailing to Villamora has been a break," Barbara interjected curiously.

"A break from implementing systems that change the way people and companies operate, yes, alright a different set of stress levels that stimulate adrenaline flow but different, and I appreciated not being in charge, just doing what Peter told me to do," Paul replied as he stood to make room for John to put the drinks tray on the small table. "Peter just told me that we will eat, in his normal restaurant, when we have finished this drink," John mentioned to Paul as he gently lowered the tray.

"So where is his normal restaurant," Barbara interjected inquisitively, looking directly at John as he stood upright from the low table. As John carefully handed Brenda and Barbara their wine glasses, "do you know," he paused, "I have no idea whatsoever."

"So, you both do exactly what Peter tells you to do, both on board and ashore?" Barbara asked looking at Brenda, "I would love a male crew who did that wouldn't you Brenda, especially for the next part of our trip," Barbara said pouting her lips sensuously.

"Peter has sailed thousands of sea miles, visiting many different harbours, we respect his judgment, and so what is the next part of your trip?" John asked.

Looking at each other inquisitively Brenda added, "We are hoping to get to the Canary Islands but after the Bay we feel that we may need extra crew to help with the night watches."

John placing, his hand on Paul's shoulder, quickly and firmly said, "Well they are going to your neck of the woods Paul."

"Why are the Canary's your neck of the woods Paul?" Brenda asked mildly.

"He owns an apartment on Fuerteventura."

"So, can we offer you a free ride to your apartment," Barbara said contemptuously with her index finger pressed against the middle of her lips.

"That's oh so kind, but one must question the use of the word free," Paul replied equally contemptuously with his index finger pressed against his lips. "Sorry to interrupt with a male sexist comment but do Brenda and Barbara does not have male partners that they can call on to help."

"No," was Barbara's rapid reply. "We leave them at home while we enjoy our favourite hobby, we only need an extra competent crew person of either gender, not partners who question our every move."

Feeling that this conversation was getting a little deep a little too quickly Paul asked the more dominant Barbara how she and Brenda met and how long they expected their trip to last. Barbara was quite happy to share the fact that they had been friends for several years and that they worked together. With Brenda quickly adding as she pointed an unobtrusive finger at Barbara that they had met when she had applied for a job at the company that Barbara owned and that their shared love of sailing had given them an extra conversation subject other than work.

"Yes, but if she hadn't been as good as she is at her work the company would not have grown anywhere as quickly giving us both time and money to sail when and where we like," Barbara said respectfully looking at Brenda.

John looked at them both whilst comically imitating Stan Laurel scratching his head with one hand, "If you are both on a boat mid ocean, how do you run your business."

"Technology darling, your friend Paul will tell you or maybe your illusive friend Peter used it on your trip here."

John looked at Paul inquisitively, "Satellite communications darling," Paul replied smiling along with Barbara.

"We have a mobile office on the boat, we can access as much as we could if we were in the office via the Internet and this is supported by self-motivated..."

"And rewarded," added Brenda.

"...managers at each of our locations," Barbara then lifted her glass towards Brenda who quickly raised hers and they both chinked glasses both with a broad smile.

"I am sorry to interrupt you," Peter said as he approached the table, looking at the two women chinking glasses, "but it is time to eat crew," now diverting his gaze to Paul and John.

"Yes, skipper but would you mind if we asked our two new friends who have just crossed the Bay like us, if they would like to join us?"" They are more than welcome," said Peter, looking at Barbara and Brenda furtively.

"Would you like to join us ladies?"

"We are both dying to eat in Peter's normal restaurant," Barbara agreed accepting Peter's hand as she rose from her low seat.

"I have told Carlos's tonight that these seats are too low. Unlike your crew, who listen to your every word, Carlos will probably not do anything," she continued.

"OK what have you two been saying to your lady friends about me, this could be an interesting dinner."

They all left the small bar, with Peter preoccupied telling everyone that they were eating and that they would see them later. Peter, still holding Barbara's hand, led them through several narrow lanes. "Not far now," he said looking pusillanimously at Barbara.

"Thank God," John interjected, "I'm starving."

"I think we all are," added Barbara, "and we all hope that your normal restaurant satisfies our needs."

"I am sure it will my dear," Peter replied as he let go of Barbara's hand and opened a small door next to a small window where a dim orange light shone through. Paul and John immediately looked quizzically at each other; both knew what each was thinking, related to their previous conversation. Quietly, close to Paul's ear, John whispered, "Surely not with female company." As he finished whispering there was a waft of air from the opened door containing a beguiling smell of food that everyone, except Peter, exclaimed, "Hmmmmm smells great."

"Panic over," Paul whispered looking over his shoulder as he went through the small door in front of John.

The female owner greeted Peter with a friendly hug adding in broken English "welcome back my good friend."

"It is always good to be fed by Maria my favourite restaurant owner," Peter replied still hugging the short rotund lady.

"I have brought my friends, can we feed them all," Peter questioned as he released Maria.

"But yes, but first wine," Maria replied as she scanned our faces and pointed to tables and chairs at the rear of the room with her outstretched arm.

"Well, I must say Peter, Brenda and I would never have found your normal restaurant in a million years, does Maria open it just for you?"

"No there will be more customers a little later, Maria doesn't need to advertise or put-up fancy signs as her food is known by all locals and people like me who return regularly."

During the meal they all thanked Peter for his superb choice of a place to eat and drink. They had all thanked Maria for her excellent cooking and choice of wine. Peter had asked Barbara and Brenda questions about their trip and their planned trip to the Canary Islands apologizing that they had to repeat the story that they had already told Paul and John. Barbara soon realised that yacht delivery was Peter's main source of income so she added light heartedly that she realised that offering Peter a free trip to the Canary Islands was not an offer that Peter would consider. Surprising John and Paul the most, Peter's reply was that as they were such nice ladies that the offer was tempting but that he needed to catch a flight to Nova Scotia in a couple of days' time as he had agreed to pick up a yacht and take it to the Azores. They all agreed that that trip sounded more exciting than the one that they had planned and that it should be them that should be offering crewing services to Peter. John told them all to continue to depress him, as he had to catch a flight back to England because he had to get back to work. Hearing his friend's comment Paul's brain began to race away with thought resulting in a serious question directed at Barbara. "If I did come with you to the Canaries, would I be able to use your mobile office when I was not on watch?" "But of course," Barbara happily replied, lifting, and holding her glass in front of Paul as a gesture of certification. John explained, as Maria brought a bottle of cognac to the table smiling and pointing at Peter, that Paul had to write the code for a new product he was developing. Paul added, for Barbara's benefit, that he would be writing the code on paper, but he needed to access his server to download the code and test it so hopefully he would not be using a large amount of satellite connection time.

"Does this mean you are joining us for tomorrow's trip then Paul," "Well yes Barbara, until now everybody seems to have plans except me, so yes I would be more than happy to be a crew member to the Canaries."

"Brenda and I have been looking at tides and weather and would like to set sail at 9.30am tomorrow morning," pausing she added, "as long as we don't drink anymore cognac tonight, we may be able to wake up on time."

"I will be on board at 9am."

"So, you are not coming back to the bar after we leave Maria's then," Peter questioned.

"No, I have had a great night, thank you, and enough to drink and now I must get my brain in gear for my next challenge."

"Is that writing the code or the sail to the Canaries," John asked jokingly.

"Sailing with two good looking women," Peter added with a broad smile lifting his glass, "here's to our next voyage in life."

Paul walked back to the marina with Barbara and Brenda after leaving Peter and John at the small bar where the evening had started, they all noticed that it looked more crowded than before. At Barbara's yacht Paul confirmed that he would see them tomorrow at 9am said good night and went to Obsession's berth. He could not believe how his life had changed since Rita had left him. He wondered what the future would bring, little did he know.

Paul set his travel alarm, as he had during the trip to Villamora, to waken him for his next watch, wondering if Barbara's watch system would be similar, making himself comfortable in his bunk wondering what time John and Peter would be back. Lying in his bunk, a little lightheaded due to his alcohol intake, Paul reflected on some of the night's conversations stopping when he remembered Peter's toast, here's to our next voyage in life. He turned this phrase over and over in his mind, finally dozing off to sleep assisted by the rhythmic sound of halyards clattering on yacht masts as the wind blew.

Chapter 18

Paul, unaware of the time that Peter and John had returned to the yacht, decided before he left to join Barbara and Brenda, that he would make everyone a cup of coffee. Paul felt that it could be considered as his parting gift. As he poured the boiling water into the cups he glanced at his wristwatch, oh he said to himself, it was only 8.15am. He was now concerned about Peter and John's reaction to being woken early following an arrival celebration drinking night.

"Morning Paul," was Peter's greeting as he came out of his berth pulling his waterproof jumper over his head. Paul realised that he need not have worried. "Oh, great you have made coffee, thanks," Peter added as his head popped out of the jumper. Paul realised that Peter had the same control regarding his alcohol intake as he had controlled his yacht command, he was envious.

Following coffee and goodbyes to John and Peter Paul made his way to Barbara and Brenda's yacht. When he arrived, he saw that the cabin hatch door was not open. He looked at his watch and realised that it was eight fifty-five not quite nine. So, he lifted his sailing bag aboard and sat in the cockpit. Even though Barbara's yacht was at least fifty feet, climbing aboard created a little movement in the marina berth. Paul began to look around the cockpit at the winches and the other sailing equipment that he had become quite familiar with on his trip down the Biscay on Obsession. He could see that the winches were a little different. He was trying to work out what the difference was and how he would need to use them when the cabin hatch door opened, and Barbara entered the cockpit. She was smiling as she approached Paul and gave him a brief cuddle before he could stand. "I am really glad to see you and your sailing bag," was her opening comment as she released Paul from the cuddle. "I must admit I had a sneaking feeling that you would not turn up, that you agreed to join us at a whimsical moment in our acquaintance, but I am really happy that you are here and sorry that Brenda and I were not here to greet you at the arranged time. Even though we left early, as you did, we both felt that we drank a little more than we would usually drink. We both felt, last night, that we were encouraged by your friends, well that is our excuse anyway."

Paul smiled adding, "Well Peter was up at virtually the same time as me this morning, and looking totally normal, he not only controls his yacht perfectly, but he also seems able to control his alcohol intake perfectly as well, I don't know how he does it, but I am envious." "Well, when we leave in about an hour's time you can judge how well I control my yacht as I agree I have failed as far as the alcohol is concerned."

Paul laughed, "I am sure your yacht control will be perfect. How many women can say that they navigated the Bay of Biscay, I must trust your ability, or I would not be here."

"All right, save the compliments for latter, I may need them," Barbara replied as she moved back towards the cabin entrance. "Let me show you your cabin where you can stow your bag and then I will introduce you to the yacht and her equipment."

They eventually left the berth in Villamora marina a little after 10am. Barbara's introduction was very thorough but had left Paul a shade concerned, as he had never sailed a yacht before with a mizzenmast. Barbara had told him that during the night watch she and Brenda mainly used the headsail and the mizzen sail, as they were both easy to reduce or extend depending on the strength of the wind. The other issue that she had mentioned at the same time was the proposed watch Rota. She had implied that she and Brenda would share watches from 7am until 10pm and that they would like Paul to take the watch from 10pm until 7am. Paul realised quickly that this was not the rotating three-hour watches that Peter had used and that he had been lumbered with the night watch where seeing other ships was not a problem but seeing floating debris was, plus if the weather did change for the worse the night watch needed to trim the sails single handed, as to wake the rest of the crew could only be considered as a last resort. Barbara, using her well-developed sales skills, had convinced Paul that this watch pattern would be good for him as he could work during the day on his App development after he had had a few hours' sleep. Paul realised that she had obviously avoided mentioning that she and Brenda were getting an undisturbed sleep at the normal time on land, but they had set sail now, so Paul had no option than to accept his female skipper's instructions. Whilst underway with just the roller reefing headsail and mizzen sail raised, Brenda prepared lunch, Paul until he started eating, did not realise how hungry he was following the very palatable meal last night. Following lunch, he announced, light heartedly, that as he was on nightshift tonight, he had better try and get some rest in his cabin. Barbara quickly agreed that was a good idea, adding, that they needed to start the 700-mile journey in the correct way. As he lay in his bunk Paul reflected on his day, the change of crew, a change of yacht. After evaluating how heedful Barbara had been exerting her authority Paul started thinking about Rita, comparing how subtly she exerted her authority without Paul being aware.

But now he was making his own mind up about what he should do. He started to think and analyse the code he needed for his fingerprint recognition app and dozed off to sleep. He woke with a start following a brief dream about his past life with Rita, when he had dozed in the armchair following a tiring day at work. He looked at his watch, it was nearly seven, his muddled brain suddenly realised that he was on a boat with two women, he didn't know at all well, and that his night watch started in a few hours' time. This was different from the armchair in the lounge at home. He could smell food. He got up from his bunk and ventured out into the main cabin. Brenda was busy in the galley, and she greeted Paul, "good evening, sir, your dinner will be served in ten minutes," she said with a broad smile. "Barbara is in the cockpit if you need to talk to her about the night watch."

"Thanks Brenda, yes I will have a chat, but I thought we may share cooking like we did on Obsession."

"No, I enjoy cooking and Barbara enjoys navigating so two duties you do not need to be concerned with." "So just night watch and nothing more?"

"Well, the skipper may have other duties for you as you are the only male on board," Brenda added, with a wink and an even broader smile.

"Yes, I guess there may be duties that need male strength," Paul replied as he climbed the steps to the cockpit thinking only about sailing issues.

Barbara was standing behind the wheel looking at the compass.

"Ah Paul, did you get some rest?"

"Yes thanks, but whether it will be enough to keep me awake until seven tomorrow morning I am not sure."

"I am sure we will be assisted by the good wind strength and wind direction that we have at the moment which is giving us an average speed of ten knots or so since leaving this morning, I reckon, and I need to verify that we have covered at least a hundred miles, which means if this keeps up, we will be at Lanzarote in a maximum of three days."

"Oh," was the only thing Paul could think of as a reply as his mind was working overtime on his work schedule for coding the app, will there be enough time was the thought passing through his mind when Barbara pointed left saying, "we are probably passing Rabat over there in Morocco at the moment so during the night you may well be passing Casablanca, I need to check on the chart below." Paul was impressed. Looking around him all he could see was ocean. "Rabat is the political capital of Morocco, but Casablanca has the most residents, last time it came to my attention it was about four million." "Your geographical knowledge impresses me," said Paul.

"Sailing and the geographical connections fascinate me and Brenda, so have you thought some more about your app project."

"Well yes I now know that I am going to write it in Java using Android base as it is close to Linux."

"Oh, now I am impressed and completely lost! I know how to operate our business systems plus I know that they are Windows based but that's it, I call in the anoraks when things go wrong. Oh sorry, that's probably you!"

"Well, it isn't my company, I would remember dealing with an MD like you if you were and yes in some things, I guess I am an anorak." Barbara had rapidly made him think of Rita and the fact that she had left him for David as she considered her husband to be an anorak even though it gave her a good lifestyle.

Brenda shouted from below, "It's ready come and get it." "Great I am hungry," was Barbara's loud reply as she turned three hundred and sixty degrees looking for other vessels. "Great nothing in sight that means we can all eat together; self-steering will keep her on course."

After the main meal and before the coffee was poured Barbara left Brenda and Paul and went back to the cockpit and returned saying, "that's good still no other vessels in sight, so you should have a quiet night Paul, just leave it to the self-steering gear and try not to fall asleep."

Paul immediately looked at his watch. "Oh, I am on shift in half an hour."

"On watch is the correct term on this yacht please Paul," Barbara replied as she wagged her index finger in Paul's face accompanying a broad smile, adding "I will bring you another coffee when you start your watch as I need you to stay awake and I do need to check the wind and our course before turning in."

Paul was happy at 7am when his watch finished. He had only started to look at his watch, by pressing the dial illumination button, just before 6am. It was now a quarter past seven and neither Barbara nor Brenda had come to relieve him. He did a slow three sixty look to make sure there were no vessels just before seven thirty and went below. He approached the forward cabins with heedfulness, "Hello it's nearly seven thirty."

"If you have got our coffee, leave it in the galley we will be out in a while," was Barbara's less than enthusiastic reply.

Paul quickly realised that even on Obsession the night watch made the remaining crew morning coffee and he had forgotten. He made coffee for Barbara and Brenda and poured himself a cup of water. He was tired and did not want to stimulate his body from sleeping. He could now feel his eyes were becoming rather heavy and awaited the women with jaded anticipation.

He was just about to return to the cockpit to make sure all was still clear when both Barbara and Brenda entered the main cabin.

"Night watch went to plan then Paul," Barbara enquired as she walked past Paul and up the stairway to the cockpit.

"Yes skipper," was Paul's terse reply.

"Just going to check where we are, before breakfast, which will be served by Brenda in a short time."

"Sorry my body is telling me that I need to hit my bunk, hope to see you at lunch time."

"Ok always good to listen to what your body tells you do, see you later."

Paul went to his cabin, lay on his bunk, fully clothed, and fell fast asleep.

He woke with a start not knowing where he was, being gently rocked by the motion of the yacht. He looked at the padded plastic side of his small cabin as he lay in his bunk. He felt really refreshed from his sleep. He looked at his watch and was surprised to see that it was just before one o'clock. Lunchtime he thought, as his stomach briefly grumbled. He entered the main cabin to find Brenda in the same position as she was over four hours earlier.

"Lunch will be served in a short time sir," she said with a cheeky grin.

"Oh, thank you steward," Paul replied as he sat at the galley table. "Captain Barbara is on watch and checking to see if we are still travelling in the same direction, now that the wind strength has dropped."

"Oh, that's good as I now have more time to get my coding finished, but please don't say that to Barbara, she was enjoying the wind strength, and our boat speed, you mustn't forget our Captain is one of life's achievers."

"Ok I will keep my mouth firmly closed on the subject, but I am ready to use the satellite comms link. Now do you think our Captain will mind?"

"No that was her deal with you, and she always honour her deals."

During the afternoon Paul entered all his code, adding more as he was entering it. He was luckily using a server on which he could perform some preliminary tests. He was a little surprised and very pleased that the tests went well especially as he was now using a yacht as his office. Feeling more positive about life than he had felt since Rita had left, he decided to e-mail a good contact in the mobile apps field giving him detailed information about the app and what market he felt should be approached. Logging off, he decided to go into the cockpit to thank Barbara.

After a very pleasant evening meal prepared once again by Brenda, who Paul now realised was the 'mother figure' of the crew, Paul went to the cockpit to start his watch at seven o'clock. At eight o'clock Barbara appeared with a large mug of coffee and handed it to Paul.

"Oh, thank you skipper,"

"Yes, tonight we do not want you to fall asleep and Brenda and I would like you to come below and join us in about an hour, say nine."

"Yes, Ok skipper I will make sure all is safe and clear up here and I will pop down." Paul felt that this was a nice invitation, as the previous night he could hear them chatting.

"Not before nine Paul, as Brenda and I will be having our strip wash in the forward heads."

"Ok skipper," Paul replied as Barbara was going down the cabin steps.

Paul looked at his wristwatch as he did the three-hundred-and-sixty-degree check for other vessels. Talking out loud, "Oh well all is completely clear, and it is now five minutes past nine, so below I go."

Paul went down the cabin steps and as he turned at the bottom, he realised that for the first time this voyage he could smell perfume, as he walked through the cabin past the galley the smell of perfume was stronger. They really have had a typical female strip wash and make over he thought as he arrived at the forward cabin entrance. He realised that the scented atmosphere was intoxicating, and he felt he was experiencing a mild erection. The cabin door was half open, so he peered in trying not to be intrusive. Both Barbara and Brenda were naked. Barbara was tenderly kissing Brenda. Paul retracted, helped by the movement of the yacht. Standing outside the cabin he could feel his mild erection was growing stronger, but he also felt that he needed them to realise his presence, so he coughed gently and pushed on the cabin door. As it opened Barbara was now caressing Brenda's breasts, Brenda's head was back, her eyes closed. As Paul stood in the open doorway, he could hear Brenda repeatedly saying, "Oh yes." He now realised that his erection was full on. But before he could back out of the cabin entrance and leave, Barbara grabbed his right hand and quietly said "Brenda would like you to stay and join us." Brenda leaned forward and held Paul's left hand moving it towards and placing it on the bulge in his loose-fitting trousers whilst slowly adding, "We can see and feel that you may like to." Brenda released his hand and slid her hand up underneath his loose-fitting sweatshirt. Paul did not move but watched as Barbara slowly kissed Brenda's breasts moving down her stomach stopping between her legs that had gently parted. Paul overwhelmed with the hedonistic ambience removed his sweatshirt and the rest of his clothes. Brenda slowly slid her hand down Paul's naked chest and held his erection, saying "I want you inside me now." Barbara moved and kissed Brenda's nipples. Brenda guided Paul inside her. Paul felt how soft, warm, and moist it felt as he penetrated deeply. He retracted and penetrated slowly and deeply, and he continued as Barbara kissed Brenda's mouth and Paul could see sensitive tongue and mouth transposition. As Paul penetrated, he could feel Barbara's hand caressing Brenda's clitoris he compassionately caressed Barbara's neck and shapely back and his other hand gently caressed Brenda's breast lingering at her erect nipple. Brenda's hand that had been stroking Paul's neck now firmly held his neck muscle and began to get tighter. He unselfishly concentrated on providing her with a satisfying orgasm. As rapid penetration continued, he could feel her muscles tensing and loosening, in anticipation, followed by "Yes, oh yes, yes yes," as her uncontrollable orgasmic convulsions overcame her. Barbara kissed her mouth tenderly as Paul retracted without ejaculating with his erection stiff and hard. Brenda's hand released his neck muscle and vehemently moved down his chest firmly holding his erection saying, "Yes now Barbara." Barbara lay back with her legs encompassing Paul's. Brenda guided Paul inside Barbara caressing her clitoris as Paul began penetrating and retracting whilst passionately fondling her ample breasts, Brenda continued to softly kiss Barbara, her head pushed back, and her eyes firmly closed. Paul ran his fingers through Brenda's hair stopping and tenderly massaging her neck and shoulder. Paul could now feel Barbara's muscles beginning to tense and loosen he could also feel that he was slowly moving towards his orgasm, so he closed his eyes and placed both of his hands at the top of Barbara's hips to sense her tensing movements. His penetration became quicker as he felt her muscles tensing more quickly. Both of her hands gripped Paul's shoulders and her grip tightened as her orgasm began, "Mmmmmm, Mmmmmmmm, Mmmmmmm," became louder and higher in tone. Her loud declarations and her vibrant body movements took Paul to his climax shouting "Oh Yes." Barbara lay lifeless as Paul finally retracted, Brenda moved across to Paul and tenderly kissed him on the lips, finishing she looked him directly in the eyes saying, "We are glad you joined us!"

"So am I," was Paul's nodded reply, adding "but now I suppose I must continue with my night watch," as he picked up his clothes and left the cabin.

Paul decided rapidly that he needed to get to the cockpit to make sure there were no other vessels close. As he did his three sixty-degree sweep he redressed, he was glad that there was nothing to be concerned about. He sat in the cockpit looking vaguely at the wind direction and how the sails were trimmed but thinking and asking himself the question, "Did that really happen and how the hell did I last so long without coming in such an unprecedented sexually stimulating situation?"

He looked at his wristwatch it was nearly ten o'clock. He decided that the headsail the mainsail and the mizzen sails needed to be tightened as the wind had shifted a little and the rig needed to be closer hauled. As he was trimming the sails and checking the wind tell tails, making sure they were not over tight, Barbara appeared with a cup of coffee. She stood in the cockpit looking at the wind direction and how Paul had trimmed the sails and looking him in the eyes, "I must admit Paul you are a real fast learner, but not only in sailing."

Taking the cup Paul returned the smile adding, "well it is always good when the crew work as a team." They both giggled.

"Paul, I have a confession," Barbara was looking down at the yacht's compass but not reading it.

"In the previous coffee that I brought for you I added a crushed blue pill, I am sorry."

Paul began to rapidly nod his head.

"We didn't know how you would react and as you now know I do not like things to fail so we both agreed selfishly that a blue pill was a good direction."

Paul continued to nod his head but more slowly now as he considered Barbara's confession. After what Barbara felt was a long time Paul looked Barbara in the eyes, "with my life prior to these two sailing trips I believe that your navigation and course setting avoided any unknown obstacles, so thank you."

"Great, I agree with you Paul, this crew has bonded as a real team." Paul felt that even though he had just witnessed Barbara having an orgasm that the skipper and boss had returned.

Paul sat in the cockpit looking at how the sails were trimmed and looking through the darkness for approaching vessels, but his thoughts were turning over what had happened earlier. Paul realised that sitting alone on night watch in the dark his brain went into overdrive. This was good when he was developing his new App, but now all he could think about, and analyse, was what had happened with Barbara and Brenda. His brain juggled with other situations. Would a woman in his situation describe what had happened as sexual harassment? He could not suppress a chuckle, could he describe what had happened as sexual harassment or maybe even rape? Was what had happened against his will? He chuckled again as he remembered that he had removed his own clothes! He frowned and nodded his head as he remembered that all his actions were generated by Barbara surreptitiously giving him a drug. He chuckled some more realising that he had never, in the past, been able to keep performing for so long, in a very erotic environment, which he reflected, would have satisfied Rita. His light-heartedness was instantly withdrawn as he thought that David might have been satisfying his wife that very night! His thoughts were reconciled as he contemplated the fact that he had been unfaithful with two women, at the same time. But he knew that all he had done with these two women had sex with them after being given a libido stimulant, all he ever did with Rita was make love with her. He could not stop thinking that his life had recently changed so much, a couple months ago could he ever have imagined that he would be where he is right now!

Chapter 19

The remainder of the trip resumed as normal with no more extra duties for Paul, for which he was extremely grateful. Barbara and Brenda did not mention the stimulated episode again for which Paul was even more grateful. On reflection he felt even more embarrassed as he had obviously satisfied their needs but why could he not satisfy Rita's needs. As he sat in the cockpit looking for other vessels to avoid and checking the sail trim, he often drifted into deep thoughts about how people treated each other. He realised he had been used by Barbara and Brenda. Had he been used by Rita and moreover is Rita using David right now, do women have self-rewarding agendas, do men have self-rewarding agendas as well. He realised that these night watches were too long on one's own now he had finished the fingerprint app. He knew this would be the last one after checking the charts with Barbara earlier before his night watch and that during the day tomorrow they should be arriving at Lanzarote.

They arrived in the Lanzarote marina early afternoon; Paul had woken as he heard the boat engine start as they prepared to enter the marina. During the voyage they had shared what their intensions were when they arrived in Lanzarote. Barbara had jokingly said that the fare to his apartment was still no charge when Paul said he would take the ferry to Fuerteventura. Barbara said that she intended to leave the yacht in Lanzarote as it would be a good place to continue to sail from to discover all the Canary Islands and that they would return to running their business back home soon after arrival.

Paul went by bus to the south of the Island and caught the ferry to Corralejo, a town north in Fuerteventura, he then caught another bus to Puerto de Rosario and walked to his apartment. When he arrived, he realised that this was a stupid decision because he did not have a key. He decided that he needed to call Claire, the local person who Rita had organised to clean the apartment and wash bed sheets and towels when Paul and Rita had stayed there, she was surprised to hear he was on the island and agreed to meet him at the apartment to give him the spare pair of keys that Rita had asked her to get cut.

"No Rita, so, you are having a break on your own," was Claire's opening greeting, followed by "Rita usually lets me know what flight you are arriving on so that I can make sure the beds are made etcetera." Paul smiled, "Rita has left me, and I sailed to Lanzarote with two women who needed a crew, so do not worry I will make my own bed as Rita has made hers."

"Oh," was Claire's initial reply, "too much information for a local, we do things more slowly here on Fuertes," she added as she gave Paul the spare keys.

"I have only one business reason to return to the UK so I do not know how long I will stay; I will call you when I leave and leave the spare keys on the kitchen table."

"OK, thanks, if you need to talk more about it give me a call and we can meet for a drink," Claire replied as she felt that this change could mean she was going to lose her job looking after their apartment.

Chapter 20

David decided to go to work even earlier the following day, so he told Rita the night before, he explained that he had an issue to deal with that he needed to deal with before other employees arrived.

"Oh, mum I forgot to give this letter from the head mistress yesterday."

"Oh, so you have been a bad schoolgirl then miss goody two shoes."

"No mum I am still miss goody two shoes."

Janet wondered, as she opened the letter, what the head mistress needed to write to her for.

"Oh," she said aloud as she read the letter, "what does Ms McLennan have to say mum."

She wants me to give the sixth form another talk on applying to join the police force when they consider their career when leaving and after university.

"Oh, not that again."

"Why did you say that darling."

"Last year, when you did it, all I got from some of the other students, mainly the rough boys, was don't tell her anything you may get arrested my mummy."

"You didn't tell me."

"No, I know, I am rather proud that my mum is a police inspector solving crimes and keeping us safe from the rough boys when they are older, I love what you do mum, so do my close friends."

"Oh, thank you darling, I didn't know you thought about my job that much, as you know I am not allowed to talk about what I do that much."

"Yes, but I have guessed that what you are working on at the moment is not too serious because you have found time to take me and pick me up from school for a couple of weeks."

Janet smiled and chuckled a little and thought she could tell Julie the type of case she was working on now.

"Yes darling, I am working on a fraud case now so I can fit it around my family life as it is about understanding how companies are trading, not people's criminal actions. Even though the people are committing a serious crime taking someone else's money."

"Oh, I like fraud cases as I see more of my mum."

"I am glad you approve; I will tell the Superintendent."

Chapter 21

Rita's office was busy as month end approached. Rita opened her bag where she kept the mobile phone that David had given her, she rang his mobile by pressing the button he had set up.

"Hello darling," was the immediate reply, "lovely to hear your gorgeous afternoon voice, did you just call to hear my voice?"

"Well yes and no," Rita replied, "I am afraid I am going to be late home tonight I have got lots of things to do before the month closes today, so I will be taking the latter train that will get me to the station at around seven thirty," as Rita said this she felt a cold chill as she thought about her receiving calls like this from Paul, *is my job becoming that important* ?

"I know your job means a lot to you and that you are obsessed with getting it right, so I will pick you up at the station at seven thirty and take you to our favourite restaurant for a nice meal to end your busy month."

"Oh thanks, that sounds great, I will try not to be late but will call your mobile if the train is delayed."

David was disappointed that he had agreed to this so easily, but he knew how much Rita's job meant to her, and he realised he had left early this morning without Rita. He also knew that he was going to leave his office a little early tonight as the number of questions from the auditors had increased so he had told them earlier that he had an appointment with his GP at five o'clock tonight. He felt stressed that the questions were getting too close to the trade he did with Phoenix.

He would have been even more stressed if he had known that the Chief Auditor had contacted the police and had been assigned Inspector Janet Mackay to investigate two trading companies, Hammit and Phoenix.

David left his office and walked down the main street heading for the main line station not taking the usual route to meet Rita at her office. He was really surprised that there were so many people around in the early afternoon and he realised that without Rita he was now not so concerned about who he might meet on the walk to the station, as he and Rita had been, since she had left Paul. He started thinking about the number of his old acquaintances who had not been in contact, could he bump into any of these as a lot of them worked in London. He also wondered what would happen if he ever bumped into Paul, he has contracts with different companies in London. He had taken every precaution to not be anywhere at home where he had any possibility of meeting Paul. He realised that Paul must hate him but felt that if he had looked after his lovely wife more lovingly, she would not have been tempted to seek love elsewhere.

Luckily, he had not seen anyone he knew as he reached the main line platform, he walked past the first couple of carriages scanning their occupants, he felt he was acting like a foreign spy trying not to be noticed. He entered the third carriage, still scanning, as he took a seat. During the journey he could not stop thinking, how long will it be until he and Rita would be accepted back by their old friends. He nearly missed his stop trying to analyse ways to contact old friends that they would accept.

He parked in the short drive behind Rita's new car. As he walked through the front door, he could smell Rita's presence by her perfume and body lotion he knew there was enough time, before he needed to be at the station to pick her up, to have a shower and close shave. He picked up the mail and scanned the envelopes to assess their urgency realising that he had not been to the PO box he had for a while now.

The train was not delayed so Rita had not needed to call David. The train arrived at her station on time at seven thirty. Rita hurried out of the exit looking for David's car, as he may have needed to park in a difficult spot, but she could not see him where cars picking up passengers usually park. She thought that maybe he arrived here early and has used the short stay car park instead, so she walked in that direction, which was towards the vehicle entrance to the station, so she looked at every car that came past to see if it was David's. Rita Walked back towards the station entrance. She looked at her watch, seven forty-five, thinking it is unlike David to be this late, so she took out her mobile phone and pressed the button, it rang. Rita let the phone ring for some time before she decided that David was not going to answer. She thought that maybe he was driving, had not attached it to the car system, and therefore could not answer it. She knew it was not a long way from David's house to the station so if he was driving then he should be here soon. Rita looked at her watch again and was shocked to see that it was five minutes past eight, she felt that something serious must have happened as David was not here, had not phoned, and had not been able to answer his mobile, so she decided to take a taxi, keeping an eye open for David's car.

"Oh," she said out loud as the taxi arrived at David's house.

"Sorry madam have I done something wrong?" the taxi driver said as he parked and turned to look at Rita.

"No, sorry, I was not expecting his car to be parked in the drive." Rita paid the driver without evaluating the cost, which she usually did when using local taxis, she was more concerned about finding her key, remembering that David had told her that she should never worry about losing it as he always left the back door unlocked, and why David had not come to meet her. She eventually found her key and entered the house.

"David, David, I am home," she walked into the lounge, no David.

"David, are you upstairs?" she said in a louder voice, thinking he has got to be here his car is in the drive. She made her way upstairs to their bedroom thinking that he may have had an afternoon nap, and overslept. No David.

"David, I am Home," *I wonder if he has gone out for a walk, but he knew he was picking me up at seven thirty.* Her feet were aching, so she took off her shoes and put them by the wardrobe. She realised that she needed to have a pee before she tried to call David's mobile again.

She walked into the bathroom, "Oh no," she screamed, when she saw David laying on the floor with blood around his head.

Do I call an ambulance, with all that blood, is he still alive, I have not felt his pulse, I do not want to touch him, what would Paul do, why have I thought what he would do, come on you silly bitch call an ambulance?

She dialled 999. "Hello caller, what service do you require?"

"Ambulance, there is blood all around his head."

"Is the patient breathing?"

"I do not know I do not want to touch him."

"Is the patient breathing?"

"He is wearing his bathrobe I cannot see."

"OK caller, what is the address?"

"Broadstead, oh no Broadmore, The Willows, Broadmore Lane Broadmore."

"Thank you caller an ambulance has been dispatched, please stay on the line until the ambulance arrives. Are you near the entrance caller?"

"No, I am upstairs in the bathroom."

"Can you please make your way carefully to the main entrance as the ambulance will be with you shortly?"

" yes."

"OK, thank you."

What the hell is happening, why have I not tried to save him, why am I walking down these stairs in a house that I do not live in, oh god what should I be doing, that must be the doorbell, never heard that before, that was quick it cannot be the ambulance already, open the door you stupid bitch.

"Hello, I am the first response paramedic, where is the patient please?"

"Upstairs in the bathroom," Rita was pointing.

"Thank you madam, what is the patients name?"

"David."

"OK, thank you madam."

Rita stood by the front door as the paramedic went quickly up the stairs. She heard a siren and doors banging, then a woman and a man wearing the same uniforms as the first man entered through the front door, she just pointed up the stairs.

Oh my god, what is happening, why is he laying on the floor, why is there blood around his head, I need somebody, Paul, Lottie.

The First responder and the female who arrived later came down the stairs.

"Have you stopped his bleeding? will he have to go to hospital?"

"Can we sit down in your lounge please?" the male said as the female linked arms with Rita.

"So your colleague is sorting out David?"

"No, I am sorry madam, David is no longer alive."

Rita stared at him then looked at the female, "Yes I am sorry madam David is dead," the female added as she held Rita's arm a little tighter.

Is this some sort of scam that David has arranged to find out how much I care, no it cannot be I called 999, oh shit this is really happening, he is dead, he is dead.

"I am sorry madam our colleague in your bathroom is calling the police."

"Oh Shit Why!" screamed Rita, releasing her arm and slapping both hands over her face, "why call the police, he is dead?"

"Yes madam, we need to call the police because the circumstances are irregular."

"Irregular, how?" Rita shouted.

"I am sorry madam, your husband has a large cut across his throat, which is the cause of his death."

"He is not my husband," Rita shouted, with her head in her hands. The female ambulance crew realising Rita was in shock placed her arm around her shoulder and hugged her, saying, "I guess he was your partner." She felt Rita's head nodding in agreement, "we will stay here for a while so please try and be calm."

What the hell is happening, what the hell did I do to deserve this.

A policeman and policewoman walked through the front door which had been left open. The female ambulance crew introduced Rita to the female police officer as the patient's partner. The policeman was led upstairs by the male ambulance crew.

Chapter 22

Detective Inspector Janet MacKay was contacted by the Superintendent and told to go to The Willows, Broadmore Lane, Broadmore, immediately as a suspicious death has been reported of one of the suspects in the fraud cases, she is investigating, and that Detective Sergeant Steven Fuller has been assigned to assist and would meet her at the address. The DI and DS arrived at the address, at the same time, and both noticed a police car was outside, and the street door was wide open, so they both entered the house, "DI MacKay has arrived, hello."

"hello ma'am we are in the lounge," said the female police officer as she hugged Rita a little firmer, "this is the partner of the deceased."

"Rita Smith, yes, and the deceased is David Prichard," replied DI MacKay, looking Rita directly in the eyes.

"I have not told anybody my full name, so how do you know it?"

"You run a company, called Phoenix, which we have been investigating."

"No I do not, I have never heard of a company called Phoenix, I work in London for a company called Lombard."

This is like a film you watch on TV, what the hell is happening, why the hell does she think I have anything to do with a company, what was it called, if David is dead what the hell do I do now.

The DI having been to the bathroom re-enters the lounge.

"I am sorry Mrs Smith I have to make this house a crime scene, can you please find somewhere else to stay locally as we will need to question you in more detail."

"Shit a crime scene, why?" said Rita very questioningly.

"David has died from a deep throat cut, we need to investigate how and why."

"So, you think someone may have cut his throat?"

"We must investigate all possibilities Mrs Smith."

DI MacKay asked the policewoman, comforting Rita, if she knew if the bathroom had been disturbed in any way if the ambulance crew had removed anything, the policewoman said she did not think so as it was the ambulance crew who had called the police because they were concerned about the cause of death.

Paul sat on the balcony, in the cooler evening sun, drinking a Tropical beer, a brand he loved when visiting Fuerteventura, when his mobile phone rang and vibrated. He looked to see the caller identity, but it was an unknown number, he thought it might be someone regarding the fingerprint product, he had patented, as he accepted the call.

"Hello Paul, it is Rita."

"I do recognise my wife's voice, after a couple of months, why are you calling."

"David is dead, and I have got to get out of the house."

"Oh," was Pauls terse reply.

"The police Inspector has made this house a crime scene."

"Shit, a crime scene, what the hell has happened, are you alright."

"Yes, David is dead in the bathroom and his throat has been cut."

"Oh, I can't say that that had not crossed my mind in the past, so what do you want?"

"The inspector has told me to find somewhere local to stay, as they need to question me further."

"You didn't do it did you?"

"No, I found him."

Paul's hate for David dissipated, slightly, the care for his wife increased as he felt she must be deeply shocked finding a dead body with a cutthroat.

"OK how can I help, I am guessing you would like to come home?"

"Yes, if you will let me."

"Only one problem, or it may be an advantage, I am at the apartment right now, so the house is empty, so if you still have your key, I have not changed the locks, you can let yourself in, and tell the Inspector that this is where you used to live before you left your husband, sorry darling, yes, use our house."

"Thanks Paul, when are you coming home?"

"I wasn't for a while but now I will check the flights tomorrow."

"Oh great, sorry but I need you."

"Sorry, no comment."

As Paul ended the call. He picked up his beer and gazed at the rippling swimming pool in the centre of the complex thinking,

Yes, I hated the bastard for taking Rita but who the hell would kill him, maybe he was a shit to other people as well, oh, shit I am glad I am here otherwise her Inspector would be making me a prime suspect, comforting Rita after his death is not going to be easy, I could have killed him easily.

After getting the body transferred to forensic pathology DI MacKay and DS Fuller performed a detailed investigation of the bathroom, where DS Fuller found a cut throat razor by the side of the bath and put it in a plastic bag to send for fingerprint testing, and DI MacKay decided that David Prichard had been shaving as the screw top of the shaving foam had not been replaced, even though there was no shaving cream on the face of the body. They agreed that there were no other items in the bathroom that needed to be considered. They both checked other rooms in the house. Even though it was not connected to David Prichard's death DI MacKay found documents related to Phoenix trading, in a file in a desk filing draw.

Chapter 23

Without thinking what she was doing Rita opened the door of the car she had originally driven to David's house and slowly drove home. She was still dazed at what had happened and could not wipe the picture of David laying on the floor, from her memory. She arrived home and put her key in the familiar front door lock. As she opened the door she shuddered, smelling the familiar smell, she leant against the closed front door and started to cry uncontrollably. She went to the kitchen, found a glass in the cupboard she had decided, in the past, was the best place to keep glasses, filled it with cold water and sat at the kitchen table and began drinking, but still crying. The familiarity of the kitchen brought a degree of relaxation, and her crying slowed down. She looked at the familiar kitchen clock and was shocked to see that it was passed midnight, she knew that she needed to try to sleep so she went to Lottie's room as it felt more secure.

DI MacKay arrived early in the morning, Rita had just made a pot of coffee and offered her a cup which was accepted, as they sat at the kitchen table. The DI explained that this was going to be an interview of two parts, the first being the lead up to discovering David's body and the second part being her involvement in the Phoenix trading company, adding that she looked a little more composed today to explain these two issues.

Rita explained that she had met David and his wife many years ago, as he was a friend of her husband Paul, and that she had always thought he was attractive. She continued the story leading up to her leaving her husband and going to live with David. The DI now asked if she could give a detailed account of the day, she discovered David's body. Rita gave as detailed account as she could as the DI was taking notes. The DI followed by asking about Rita's family's reaction to her leaving her husband. Rita looked straight at the DI with a frown and lips pressed tight and raised.

"Why, do you think my family had anything to do with David's death."

"In these circumstances we must investigate all possibilities, we know Mr Smith is now in Fuerteventura so DS Fuller has checked the flights from Fuerteventura to establish if Mr Smith had an outgoing and return flight on the same day, he is currently visiting Mr Jeffrey Johnson and Mr and Mrs Green to establish their movements on the day, can you give me names of any other people who may have been involved."

Rita's eyes were wide open.

"He is questioning my family, holy shit, they didn't even know David, and Lottie is heavily pregnant this can't be happening, and no I don't know anyone else."

"I am sure DS Fuller will consider the individual circumstances and question appropriately, thank you for your details on the day, I now need to question you regarding your involvement with Phoenix."

"I have never heard of Phoenix until you mentioned it yesterday."

"Well, how is your signature on a number of Phoenix documents including the Phoenix bank account, and a bank account in your name."

Rita had opened the kitchen table draw and taken out a pen and writing pad which she put on the table and signed her name, twisted the writing pad around to show the DI.

"That is my signature, how does that compare to the ones you are telling me are on these Phoenix documents."

The DI glanced at the writing pad then took a document out of her bag and placed it aside the writing pad.

"The signatures are the same, you must have signed these documents."

Rita could feel anger building up.

"What can I say to convince you, I have never signed anything to do with this company called Phoenix, my partner is dead and now you are telling me about something I have never done or heard of."

The DI took another document from her bag and placed it on the table in front of Rita.

"Do you recognise this document."

"Yes, it is the document I signed, at Reception, at David's company, when I visited him on Fridays."

The DI showed Rita that the document was multi part and her signature would have been on a blank A4 document attached to a covering document registering a visit to David Prichard. I have questioned the receptionist and he told me that David Prichard gave him these documents when he expected quests, which was primarily you Mrs Smith.

Rita's eyes widened and her chin dropped, her hand clenched her chin and she started shaking her head from side to side.

The DI watched without continuing questioning and waited for a while before adding.

"I feel that this has been a shock."

Rita simply nodded her head with her eyes fixed on the document in front of her.

"It is now becoming more obvious that David Prichard may have completed the blank part of these documents to support trading to and from Phoenix and that you were not aware of this, but I had to be sure that you had no involvement."

Rita made eye contact with the DI as tears started to roll down her cheeks and sobbing, she said.

"He was bloody using me, and I thought......."

Rita stopped talking as her crying increased and she lurched forward with her head in her hands.

The DI placed her hand on Rita's shoulder.

"I am sorry Mrs Smith this information has obviously shocked you a great deal, the good news is however that I am totally convinced that you had nothing to do with David Prichard's embezzlement activities and that you have no claim over the large amount of money in the bank account that he set up in your name."

"Oh, for fucks sake, he set up a bank account in my name as well."

"Yes, using the address we were at yesterday."

"So that is why he used a lockable letter box, so that I could not see any letters with my name, how was he embezzling."

"Simply, he was transferring good deals to Phoenix and bad deals to the company he worked for, the auditors are quantifying these deals and they tell us that the company will most certainly organize bailiffs to reclaim their losses from David Prichard equity which following my investigation will now include the bank account in your name."

"How did I not realise he was living a lie, how could I be so blind, and he was using me to support it, I knew I did not know enough about how he made all the money he spent."

The mainline phone rang, and the DI nodded towards the phone to emphasise that it was acceptable for Rita to answer it.

"Hello Darling."

"Mum, what are you doing there, I expected dad would be home from his sailing trip by now, are you back together then?"

"Dad is flying back from Fuerteventura to support me."

"Oh, why do you need support mum."

"Because yesterday I found David dead in the bathroom with his throat cut."

"Oh shit, we didn't like it that you left dad for him, but we wouldn't wish anyone dead."

"Enough of that, are you and baby OK."

"Yes, we are doing fine thanks."

"Great, stay that way. I am told by a Lady Detective Inspector, who is here with me right now, that her male Detective Sergeant will be visiting you and grandad soon to understand where you were when it happened."

"So, they think somebody killed him."

"Yes, at the moment."

"Do you want me to come round."

"Yes, I could do with a cuddle, could you ring grandad and warn him."

"Ok, be there soon."

Rita put the phone back in the receiver and looked at the DI.

"My daughter and her husband Kevin will be coming round here soon."

"Oh, good I will tell DS Fuller," as she picked up her radio, "I can ask them where they were at the time David died."

"Your Detective Sergeant may have a problem contacting my father as he is a lorry driver and he does quiet long hours, if my daughter can contact him, he may be free to come round with them."

Chapter 24

Lottie, Kevin, and Jeff arrived at the house at the same time and were questioned by the DI and they all explained where they were when David died.

They all added that it would have been difficult anyway as they had never met him and had no idea where he lived.

DI MacKay left as the family were consoling Rita. When outside and in her car, she contacted the Forensic Pathologist, who said that the report had been sent. She immediately accessed the report and began reading, she was amazed when she read that Mr Prichard had died of an aneurism of the aorta which they assumed occurred before the throat was cut and that it was very possible that when the aneurism occurred Mr Prichard would have experienced considerable pain causing involuntary physical reactions. She immediately contacted the fingerprint unit and was assured that it was only Mr Prichard's fingerprints on the cutthroat razor.

She thought about this additional information for a while and concluded that there was no third-party involvement that Mr Prichard had cut his own throat when suffering an aneurism. She contacted DS Fuller to inform him. She returned to Rita's house, and the family were still there, she informed them that her investigation had concluded, as the pathologist had stated that Mr Prichard had died of an aneurism of the aorta and not a cutthroat.

Chapter 25

Rita called Paul on his mobile phone to tell him the new information and that her father, daughter, and son in law were there to comfort and help. Paul told her that he was at the airport and booked on a flight which was leaving in thirty minutes. She said that he did not need to return for her sake now, although it was very kind that he had offered. Paul replied,

"No OK, I am still coming back, as our daughter's baby is due soon."

He paused,

"You can return the favour though; you can pick me up at the airport in five hours' time."

Rita agreed and Paul gave her the flight details, a procedure that had happened before when Paul had visited the apartment without Rita.

Rita arrived at the airport and parked in a similar place to where she had before. Paul met her and they walked to her car with conversation limited, but Rita telling Paul that their daughter and son in law had bought a new house in Amberton and how the sale of their property had happened. Then Rita eventually said,

"You look very well,"

"Yes, that was the sailing trips, not my time at the apartment."

"Sailing trips, Lottie told me about the trip with John was there another then."

Paul hesitated before answering,

"Yes, I was crew on another yacht from Portugal to Lanzarote."

"Oh, did John join you."

"No,"

"Who was that with then."

Paul did not answer immediately and luckily Rita was distracted from the conversation through traffic issues,

"So, who was that with."

"It was a couple of people we met at the marina in Portugal."

"What a man and wife."

Paul hesitated again before answering,

"No, it was two women."

"Oh, just you and two women, where they nice looking women."

The conversation continued with Paul aware that this was not the time or place to share all details about the trip and what had happened with Brenda and Barbara. Paul managed to evade direct questions by tactfully asking Rita why she had had a relationship with David.

"I was excited about being considered attractive and desired again, but didn't realise until the DI told me that the bastard was using me to support his embezzlement activities as well as having his way with me." She paused then added, "Oh sorry darling."

"So, if he hadn't died, he would have been arrested and you would have been implicated as well."

"I had not considered that, yes you are right."

"I have learnt during our separation that you can't fully trust anyone."

"So, you had a problem with someone like I had with David."

"Sort of."

They arrived at their house and the conversation ended as they both were thinking about entering the house together as they had for many years before the separation.

"I have been sleeping in Lottie's room, I didn't think it was right to use our bed."

"Oh, I sort of understand, but you can sleep in our bed tonight if you want."

"What with you."

"Yes, I have realised a lot of things since you went, mainly that I did not pay enough attention to our physical life together like regular cuddles, so can I please have a cuddle."

Rita looked at him with a facial frown then opened her arms and moved closer to him. They had a lengthy cuddle.

"Does this mean that I am forgiven."

"Does this mean that I am forgiven for not being an attentive husband."

They both starred each other directly in the eyes and kissed.

"I will not be spending time working on customer projects anymore."

"Oh, does this mean you want to live on my income and be a house husband?" Rita laughingly replied.

"No, I now have a regular income."

Paul explained the fingerprint app that he had developed whilst sailing to Lanzarote with Barbara and Brenda and that several companies had leased it and that he was sure that this would provide a regular income for some time.

Rita looked surprised.

"So, we can spend more time together, shall I give up my job as well then."

"That will be your choice."

"Yes, I will."

That will help me to forget meeting that bastard and dumping this lovely husband, we need to celebrate this strange reunion, where is the wine.

"I am going to open a bottle of wine to celebrate our reunion."

"Great, I will drink to that."

They finished the bottle and went to bed together.

Chapter 26

"Well, we have been sitting here, on our settee in our new home, for nearly half an hour," Lottie said looking at her watch, "you my lovely darling, have supplied me and our unborn family, with so much sweet tea that instead of our baby wanting to come out into this wonderful world I am afraid that it's the tea that wants to be first." Kevin chuckled; his anxiety relieved a little as Lottie's statement sounded a little more cheerful. He also thought that this may have been a result of the phone call she had received from her mother and father to tell her that they were back together again.

"Do you need me to help you to the toilet," Kevin said holding Lottie's hand tenderly again.

"What? so that you can manage the 'outs' as well as the 'ins'?" Lottie replied laughing.

"No darling, just that in our new home, unlike our old one, the toilet is now upstairs."

"Very considerate of you sweetheart, but I have climbed stairs before, even yesterday, to reach our apartment from the ground floor."

"Ok, I am being too sensitive," Kevin said as he helped Lottie to get up from the settee.

Kevin stood at the bottom of the stairs as Lottie went up them. When she reached the top Kevin went back into the lounge and picked up the cups and saucers and took them into the kitchen. He was washing and drying them, with a tea towel he found in a box labelled 'KITCHEN' when there was a knock at the front door. On his walk to the front door Kevin couldn't stop thinking how organised Lottie had been with the move, all the boxes were labelled with which room they should be put into.

Kevin opened the front door. He was faced with a smiling middle-aged lady.

"Hello, sorry to bother you so early I realise that you have only just moved in, but I have a day off work today so I thought I would say welcome, I am Mary your next-door neighbour."

"Hello new next-door neighbour, please come in," Kevin replied to smiling shaking Mary's hand. As Mary entered the house Lottie was coming down the stairs. Kevin looked up at Lottie saying, "This is Mary our new next-door neighbour and I have invited her in for a cup of my perfect tea."

"Oh, hello Mary, it's great to meet you, we haven't had a cup of tea for ages," Lottie said laughing.

"Oh, I am sorry," Mary added. "Have all the neighbours been in to welcome you."

"No Mary it's not you or the neighbours it's Kevin because the baby has been kicking for ages and we thought that sweet tea may help."

"What is your due date," Mary enquired.

"Two weeks' time," both Lottie and Kevin said simultaneously.

"So, I guess you have both been worried about the move date, more than most people moving home would be," Mary said thoughtfully. "Arghh......." was Lottie's reply, holding her stomach whist grimacing with pain as she sat on the settee facing Mary.

"When was your last contraction," Mary enquired.

"If these are contractions, then, just half an hour ago," Lottie replied. Mary described in simple terms the type of pain Lottie was feeling and Lottie agreed with her.

"Yes, you are having contractions Lottie," Mary said confidently. "So, can you remember how your contractions felt when you had your family then Mary?" Lottie said quizzically.

"Well yes but ……"

Mary could not finish the sentence as Lottie interrupted with another "Arghhh……." holding her stomach again.

When Lottie looked in less pain Mary said, "I know that this will sound strange, from your new neighbour, who you have only just met, but can I please examine you Lotti?"

Both Lottie and Kevin looked at Mary wide-eyed. "I am a Midwife at Redford hospital, if today wasn't my day off it would be me who would be examining you when you were brought to hospital, and I would start by checking your dilation."

Directing his wide-eyed stare towards Lottie Kevin said, "Your guide really does look after you! Now I am gob smacked."

Following a brief examination Mary told Kevin to call an ambulance.

The contractions were now coming more regularly. Mary took the cushions from the settee and armchairs and made a bed on the living room floor.

"Kevin," said Mary, "please boil some water and let it cool, and please get me some towels.

"They are in the box labelled airing cupboard," Lottie gasped as the pain returned. When Kevin returned, in no time at all with the towels, Mary could sense the stress and anxiety Kevin was trying to control. "Kevin, please hold Lottie's hand and comfort her, everything is fine, there is nothing to worry about," Mary said gently and calmly.

Holding Lottie's hand Kevin whispered, "Let's pray that your guide is with you right now."

"Our Heavenly Father is always with us, especially when we pray," Mary added looking with strength into Kevin's concerned eyes.

Chapter 27

The ambulance arrived at the same time as Lottie gave birth to a baby boy, with Mary's professional help.

"Hi Mary," said the ambulance crew, "setting up alternatives to Redford hospital, now, are we?"

Everybody laughed.

"Hi John, Hi Sandy," Mary replied to the ambulance crew as she listed actions, she had for Jill her colleague midwife, who was on shift at the hospital today.

"So, do we have a name for our new neighbour," Mary asked Lottie as Lottie held her new-born wrapped in one of the towels Kevin had found. Lottie stared at Kevin, who couldn't take his eyes off their delicate son.

"Does he look like the name we discussed Kevin?" Lottie raised her voice a little. Kevin still didn't reply, tears appearing on his unshaven cheeks. Lottie repeated the question even louder as Mary gave Kevin a paper tissue saying, "well?" looking directly at Kevin.

"Yes, he is definitely our Luke." Kevin said now looking deeply into Lottie's smiling eyes.

"Kevin, please call my mum and dad to tell them that Luke has arrived safely."

Kevin followed the ambulance to Redford hospital, as Sandy had suggested that he would probably need his car later when leaving the hospital. Sandy and Mary both realised that Kevin's thoughts were only for Lottie and Luke, and he was not thinking straight now.

"So, this is what Mary does on her days off, moonlighting midwifery with next door neighbours, eh?" Jill said laughing with Lottie and Kevin.

"Thank God Mary was there." Kevin replied.

"That's our Mary, always seems to be where she's needed most at the right time, she says she must be guided," Jill added.

Looking at Kevin and smiling Lottie said, "So Mary has a guide as well."

"OK, as a proud new father there is more to this guide thing than I have ever previously considered," Kevin replied as he gently touched Lottie's hand that was wrapped around Luke.

"Sometimes I think that I should be a confirmed Christian like Mary," Jill said thoughtfully.

"She says that the Holy Spirit is always with her guiding her, and in this job we all need guidance and help."

"So, your guide is the Holy Spirit then," Kevin said to Lottie without his usual sarcasm.

"I guess so, I've never thought of it like that though, I always thought that Holy things were for the bible bashing types," Lottie replied looking alternately at Jill and Kevin.

"Well, Mary isn't a bible basher, she does go to the church on Sundays when she's not on shift but with all the reading we need to do, to keep up to speed in this job, I can't see how she can find the time," Jill said whilst checking Lottie's blood pressure.

Kevin stayed with Lottie and Luke if the hospital staff would allow, he tenderly kissed them both before leaving. He drove home carefully, as demanded by Lottie, and after making the bed in their new home and setting the alarm clock for 6.30am fell fast asleep.

The alarm woke Kevin out of a deep sleep, although still a little dazed; he got out of bed quickly as he knew he needed to spend a lot of time getting their new home as comfortable as possible for when Lottie and Luke came home.

After tidying and unpacking as much as possible, Kevin was back at the hospital at 9.30am. When he walked into the maternity ward Kevin saw Mary and went and thanked her for all her help.

"That's what neighbours are for isn't it," Mary laughingly replied following quickly with, "I hope that you have got everything sorted out at home because you can take Lottie and Luke back with you in an hour or so."

"Oh fantastic," Kevin said very excitedly.

Kevin walked down the ward with his eyes fixed on Lottie and Luke, as Luke was being breast-fed. Kevin and Lottie had discussed feeding before Luke was born and had agreed that natural feeding was best if Lottie could manage it. Kevin knew it was early days but to witness his family doing it, took his breath away.

"Heck," was Lottie's word as the three of them entered the living room on their return from hospital.

"You only had a little time, late last night and early this morning to make our new home this tidy darling, it looks great," Lottie added. "Teamwork helped, your box labelling was the key factor, so thank you mummy," Kevin replied kissing both Lottie and Luke.

Lottie was really pleased to see her mother and father later that day and she felt relaxed that they appeared to be happy with each other.

During the days that followed Lottie organised the home slowly to fit her needs caring for Luke. They both wanted Luke's cot in their bedroom, they had agreed that this was not going to be permanent, but they wanted to share these early days of Luke's life as a family.

Chapter 28

Lottie and Kevin were having a cup of tea when there was a knock at their front door. Lottie opened the door to a lady wearing a dog collar.

"Sorry to bother you, my name is Joyce, I have just called to say hello and welcome to Amberton. As you can see from the way that I am dressed, in this very fashionable collar, that I am your local Anglican Vicar at St Peter's church here in the village."

"Please do come in, Kevin and I were just having a cup of tea, would you like to join us," Lottie asked.

"Ah, drinking tea eh, we don't need Mary, again, do we?" enquired Joyce with a board smile.

"Oh, you have heard about our arrival day then," Kevin said inquisitively.

"Yes, Mary told me, she said that her neighbourly love came a little earlier than she expected,"

"Yes, and so did ours," Kevin added quickly.

"Yes, we all love Mary," Joyce added.

"Mary told me that you have called your son Luke,"

"Yes, we both felt that he looked like a Luke when he was born," said Lottie.

"A lovely name and for me a lovely Gospel," Joyce replied.

"Ah," Lottie and Kevin said simultaneously.

"Well, I know you are Lottie and Kevin, but I don't know your surname?" Joyce asked.

Lottie and Kevin looked at each other with embarrassment, and then Kevin said quietly,

"We have two surnames; we are not married."

Realising their embarrassment Joyce quickly said, "please don't be embarrassed, in front of me or any other villagers, all we care about is that as Luke's parents you raise him in a caring loving environment."

She then added, smiling as she left the house, "Now I am really not touting for business, but if you ever do decide to get married or have Luke baptised, here's the telephone number of the vicarage, please do call me."

When he closed the door after saying goodbye to Joyce, Kevin said something to Lottie that he never believed he would hear himself say. "She is such a real person I would really like to be married, to you, by her."

"Yes, and so would I," Lottie replied without hesitation.

"Well let's call her and make the arrangements," Kevin concluded.

"Yes."

Jeff Johnson = Rita's father

David Prichard = Lover/friend of Paul

Paul Smith = husband

Rita Smith = Wife

Lottie Green = Daughter

Kevin Green= son in law

Janet Mackay = police inspector

Steven Fuller = police sergeant

Ms Mclennon = Head mistress

Julie Mackay = Inspector Mackay daughter

THE END